# Confessions of a Golf Pro

D1532280

## By Andrew Wood

**The book is in not endorsed or affiliated with the PGA of America, UK or in fact the PGA of any country!**

ISBN: 0-692-97483-0
ISBN-13: 978-0-692-97483-4

# DEDICATION

**This book is dedicated to all my amazing PGA professional friends past and present including:**

Gwil Hardiam, Shaun Ball, Kevin Short, Peter Baker, Rick Danruther, John McNair, Scott Wyckoff, Rudy Virga, Garith Jones, Rick Peters, Larry Starzel, Mark Wood, Chris Wainright, Randy Robins, John Reger, Russ Libby, David Frost, Dick Pearce, Randy Mudge, Dr, Gary Wiren, Rod Cook, Chuck Cook. Jim Mclean, Charlie King, Kevin Strom, Lorie Wilkes, Joey Rassett, Larry Murphy, Randy Shannon, John Twissell, Bill Mory, Rich O'Brian, Greg Thoner, Jeff Smith, Rich Smith, Derrek Crawford, Duke Bowen, Mark Baron, Gareth Jones, Chris Holmes, Jeremy Nichols, Dennis Walters, Aaron Gleason, Jeff Smith, Mac Hood, Rick Danruther, Jerry Moore, David Bauchman, Johan Tumba, Graham Stewart, Mike Stevens, Gary Gilleon, Anthony Mocklow, Jeremy Udovich, Kevin McKinley, Scott Seifferlin, Jerry Springer, Ronnie Springer, Rich O Brian, Ira Kramer, Brian Boeling, Doug Bell, Tom Ronshaw, Micheal Todd, Donna White, Ken Green, Jeremy Dale, Daniel Webster, Simon Knabl, David Ogrin, Mike Warobick, Paul Adams, Shaun Finley, Doyle Moffit, Bob Devitz, Brian Jolley, Rob Vaga, Nigel Bowerman, Marc Brady, Jon Turner, Noel Allen, Blaze Grinn, Thom Miller, Jeff Gandee,

Scott Schneider, Joe Kruse, And the thousands more whose names I have inadvertently forgot at 11.32 pm after five Stella's and 14 hours at my computer.

You have all suffered enough, the truth had to come out eventually…

# CONTENTS

# ACKNOWLEDGMENTS

Thanks to Patrick Clark for his contribution to the
continued success of all my books.

# CHAPTER 1

## OPENING THE SHOP AT 6 A.M STILL DREAMING OF AUGUSTA GLORY

My name is Jerry Sawyer, I'm 46 years old, six feet tall, in decent shape, better than average looking and I can still shoot the occasional round under par, albeit from the member tees. All I ever wanted to be was a golf pro, and now of course, I am.

One should always be careful what one wishes for!

When I dreamed of being a golf pro as a youngster, I dreamed of green jackets, traveling the fairways of the world and sipping champagne from a claret jug. Not folding shirts, running summer brat camps and selling Mars bars.

Unfortunately, lack of talent held me back from a career on the PGA Tour, I was good, just not good enough. Now I have 521 bosses, a tiny box-filled office, work six days a week all summer and make less money than the bag boy. Seriously he works the bag drop in the mornings and a high-end restaurant at night, clearing $1,000 a week in cash plus his two minimum wage checks, and he's only 19. Works less hours too.

"Where did it all go wrong?" I wonder to myself as I pull into the parking lot just after 6 am in my, five-year-old Dodge Charger, another throwback to my teenage dreams that wasn't living up to expectations!

To add to my middle-aged joy the President of the club, Hal Formby, who bears a startling resemblance to Judge Smails of Caddyshack fame is trying every trick in the book to make me quit or have me fired!

I open up the pro shop, deactivate the alarm, turn on the lights, switch on the coffee pot and fire up the computer. Here we go… another day in the life of a golf pro begins.

Check down:

Read the right-wing news on Fox first.

Glance at left-wing news on CNN followed by the Telegraph in London to give me some real news and an objective perspective on world events.

Check my Facebook page. Just a couple of comments from friends on my selfie pic in yesterday's pro-am.

Check the club's Facebook page. Thankfully most of the members haven't figured out how to use the message feature yet!

Open my email. 145 messages mostly spam.

Review the real emails starting with emails from my esteemed members.

**Email #1**

Sender Mrs. Stein

Jerry:

"Why don't you carry Lacoste ladies wear in the pro shop, all the best clubs do!"

Gloria

**My Reply:**

Dear Mrs. Stein:

The reason I don't you carry Lacoste ladies wear in the pro shop is because neither you nor the other members of "The Tribe" in your ladies group are going to want to pay $95 for a golf shirt! So, they would sit in my inventory all year until I write them down 60% in November. Then you and the cheap bastards you play with will scoop them up for $20 less than I paid for them!

**Jerry Sawyer**

**PGA Professional**

Of course, that's not the reply I sent. Hey, after all, I've been to PGA business school, it's just the reply in my head and my heart.

**What I actually sent was:**

**Mrs. Stein:**

Thanks for letting me know of your interest in Lacoste ladies wear. Although I personally love the brand, unfortunately, we do not have enough volume to open an account with this wonderful brand. If you tell me what styles you like from their online store www.Lacoste.com, I'll be happy to talk with their rep and see if we can do a custom order. With your member discount of course!

At your service ☺

**Jerry Sawyer**
**PGA Professional**

**Email #2**

Sender: Doc Palmer

Jerry:

Who the hell is the joker who put the flag on top of the ridge on 17, yesterday? I four-putted from six feet, and as you know, I am one of the best putters in the club. Please instruct the ground staff in the basics of golf and flag positioning. This is not the first time I have had to bring this to your attention.

Doc Palmer

**My Reply:**

Doc I hear you, but that red-headed, Scottish, twat of a greenkeeper we have, thinks it funny to piss off the rich members, who he detests for hacking up his precious grass, by always positioning at least one flag in a ridiculous location every day. I have indeed mentioned this to him several times, but the truth is since he is married to the president's daughter he just doesn't give a flying fuck what you think or what I tell him!

Jerry

**And what I actually, end up sending…**

**Doc:**

I don't believe you ever had a four-putt in your life! In fact, I can't even find anyone who's ever seen you three-putt, never mind four-putt, but I'll have a word with Angus nonetheless.

**Email #3**

Sender: Joe Tomson

Jerry:

Why are the greens so abominably slow?

**My Reply:**

Joe:

The only thing around here that abominably slow is your group's pace of play. You call your group the "Tigers." The "Wounded Snails" would be more apt!

**And what I actually sent...**

Joe:

According to the Super they were running ten on the stimpmeter yesterday. How fast should I tell him you like them?

**Email #4**

Sender: Sally Tomson (Yes, they are married)

Jerry, must we shave the greens so low that you can't even keep the ball on the green. IT is supposed to be fun, you know?

**My Reply:**

Sally old girl, shaved is "in." Go Brazilian!

Then I got an image in my head quick-opted for a cut and paste job for the actual reply...

Mrs. Tomson:

According to the Super they were running ten on the stimpmeter yesterday. How slow should I tell him you like them?

FYI: Your husband thinks they are too slow, maybe have a word...?

**Email #5**

Sender: Fred Stedman

Jerry:

As you may know, my wife volunteers for the local dog shelter and they are having a golf tournament to raise money. I wonder if you might donate a foursome for the raffle?

**My Reply:**

Yes, of course, I will you miserable old fuck, but it would have been nice if your wife had at least talked to me about holding the event here before she booked it at the club down the street!

**And the actual reply:**

Fred:

Of course, we would love to support your wife's efforts in such a good cause Winston (that's my Black lab), and I will be happy to donate a foursome.

Jerry

PS. Perhaps next year we could petition your good wife to hold the event here?

**Email #6**

Sender: Mrs. Goldstein

Jerry:

I am afraid the bag boys have been stealing my balls again!

**My Reply:**

Mrs. Goldstein:

Yes, they did take all two dozen of the red striped balls from your puke green golf bag. Which you left open, spilling all of them across the bag room floor. They deposited them back with all their other shiny new cousins in a big black hopper that serves as our range machine! You may not know this, but range balls are genetically engineered to make you score higher if you use them on the golf course, but we do have a buy one get one free special on a box of those pink balls the ladies all LOVE!

**What I actually sent:**

Mrs. Goldstein:

It's so hard to find good help these days, please accept my apologies. Stop by the shop and we'll get you some new ones, and maybe we can find out who keeps putting those range balls in your bag?

**Email #7**

Sender: Sid Newman

Jerry:

I think you need to have a word with the tournament committee. This year members-guest event which, as you know, is one of our Majors is scheduled a week later than normal.

This is going to cause serious scheduling problems for MANY members like me who have already made travel plans based on the traditional member-guest dates, i.e., the first week in September. One can never be sure of the weather after the first week and having the event start on the 13th is just asking for trouble. What were these people thinking?

Please have them it changed back to its traditional date ASAP as my wife and I have already booked a cruise.

**My reply:**

Mr. Newman:

I can certainly see your point I was born on the 13th and look what happened to me. I ended up as a shop pro serving a bunch of old fucks like you who complain about the sun coming up in the morning but, only on days that end in y!

As for the tournament committee, I have about as much swing there as your Rabbi does in Mecca! Perhaps you and your endless supply of sandbagging partners, who have captured no less than four of the last five member-guests, could give someone else a chance?

Enjoy your cruise and watch out for icebergs!

Your Friendly PGA Pro ☺

Jerry

### Email #8: Mrs. Hunt - Stolen Club!

Dear Jerry:

I lost my 6-iron last week somewhere on the front nine, I am shocked that no one has turned it in. I naturally assume it was stolen by a guest. Please order me a new one; I am totally lost without it. It's a Dunlop blue something!

Mrs. Hunt:

### My Reply:

I am sorry to hear of your loss, but I don't think that it's going to make making that much difference to your game since you hit every single club in your bag 115 yards, and haven't taken a lesson in the 14 years I've been the pro.

I checked online, and Arnie was still winning golf tournaments when they last made the Dunlop Blue Flash model you play. Either stop in and let me fix you up with a new set, (I have a nice set with pink grips in stock to match the balls you play) or keep checking on e-bay in the vintage club section and see if you can score one!

Best of luck,

Jerry

There are 14 in all each more exasperating than the next. They blame me for the greens, the flags, the food, the fashion choices, dates on the calendar and the cheating bastard who won last week's event with a 61 playing off 10!

But it's not all bad; there are a small bunch of good members, people that appreciate their pro, buy from the shop, take an occasional lesson and drop me a bottle or two of wine at Christmas or Hanukah since half the membership is Jewish.

The thing about the Jewish members is they tell it like is or at least like they think it is. There is no subplot or Machiavellian political subtlety like there is with every Wasp comment or request. Just simple, straightforward talk that some of my juniors take as obnoxious, but frankly I prefer. It's hard enough doing this job without having to mind read the actual question or subplot behind every seemingly polite and "harmless" request!

# CHAPTER 2

## DRESS CODE PROBLEMS

I t's 1:30 pm on Saturday. About the time the couples groups start showing up so they can end their round in perfect time for cocktails, followed by dinner.

Mr. Hannes, a successful entrepreneur in the mold of Donald Trump, shows up twenty minutes late for his one o'clock tee time.

He marches hurriedly into the pro shop with a former tour pro and his stripper girlfriend. I know that's judgmental, the truth is I have no idea what the young lady actually does for a living but a Nun she is not... although she is wearing black! In fact, she is dressed head to toe in a black. A black body suit that leaves zero to the imagination and clearly shows she has nothing on underneath.

They sign in. Heads turn, tongues wag. They hit a couple of putts and walk over to the first tee. The people there stare at this gorgeous blonde in a black catsuit and white Pumas. The pro and Mr. Hannes hit from the back tees. She moves up to the men's tees wiggles her gorgeous bum and nails it 240 down the middle with a little draw.

The men on the tee gasp with delight and cannot conceal their excitement, many for the first time in years without Viagra. The ladies with them, all north of 65, wait until she walks a few strides down the first fairway (she prefers to stretch those long legs out apparently) and immediately jump in their carts and head back to the pro shop like a posse fixed on lynching.

This I have already expected and have prepared my defense.

They literally jump from their golf carts and swarm into the pro shop like angry bees.

"What are you going to do Jerry?" they demand.

I feign ignorance, "About what ladies?"

"About that trollop on the first tee?" they spew in unison.

"I am sorry," I feign shock at their suggestion, "Do you mean Mr. Hannes' guest?"

"Yes!" they exclaim, "Did you see the way she was dressed?"

"I did indeed and went immediately to our club rules and regulations book to check whatever you call, whatever it was she was wearing but… it was not too short as they were technically long pants. It had a collar of sorts and long-sleeves so it was not a cutoff or a t-shirt. It was all black with no logos or offensive slogans. While we may need to review our policies I could not find one reason in our current club rules to request she wear different attire!"

"Are you serious?" yells Mrs. Stanton.

"I am afraid I am. As you know, Mrs. Stanton, I don't write the rules that's up to the members." I state calmly, concealing a smug smile with a look of genuine concern on my face.

They shuffle out of the shop back to their husbands who are now all watching her second shot through their range finders to see the finer points of her swing or her nipples poking through her spray-on suit in finer detail!

We would later learn she went on to shoot 75. Not bad for her first time out from the 6,500 yard tees. It turns out her father used to be head pro at one of the top clubs in New York, who knew?

After the round, Mr. Hannes showers, changes and brings her to dinner, which on Saturday night, is jackets and ties mandatory. His Jacket is new a white one covered in 1950s pin up girls. Loudmouth, I suspect. His tie matches perfectly, which is to say perfectly ridiculous, but I know he's doing it just to poke a middle finger at some of the members. She's in a short black cocktail dress and looks ravishing, while her golf pro date has a Stars and Stripes jacket also by Loudmouth. The whole thing looks like a cartoon; only they are the only ones laughing.

I am having my one drink at the bar before dining with a prospective new Assistant Manager. Once again, members shuffle up to me and whisper frantically in my ear. But once more he has outfoxed them by sticking to the letter of the club rules. Payback from previous slights and reprimands. I quietly admire him, although that's something I'd keep to myself, along with voting for Trump!

Two weeks later, after another reprimand for some minor infraction when his guest made the mistake of answering a cell phone call in the clubhouse while Hannes was on a pee break, Hannes has upped his game again.

He walks into the club wearing a new jacket adorned this time with images of topless island girls while sporting a giant sombrero he picked up in Cabo. The club manager greets him and asks him to remove his hat. Mr. Hannes calmly asks the manager if he would have asked a man to remove his hat had he been wearing a turban? The manager replies that in that unlikely event he would not have asked the man to remove his turban. Hannes continues by asking had a lady been wearing a burka would she be denied entry or asked to remove it? This was an even greater stretch of the imagination in a club that was half Jewish, but again the manager demurred that he would not.

And "Why not?" asked Mr. Hannes.

"Because it's their religious beliefs," stated the manager.

"Exactly!" announced Hannes with glee.

"Mr. Hannes, you are not going to tell me" … started the manager but was cut off mid-sentence when Mr. Hannes held up his hand and brought out a pamphlet from his jacket declaring his new faith as that of the *Mariachi Martyrs For Christ*.

"One of our strongest beliefs is that we should always cover our heads with a specific type of native headwear."

"Please," said the manager, pleading knowing how many emails and calls this would provoke.

"If you'd like to take it up with my lawyer you know where to find him, Mr. Jackson's a member. I am sorry but I must take a stand. There is no room for religious persecution in this club or in this politically correct world in which we live."

The manager shakes his head and walks off. He knows it's a battle he cannot win. That does not mean three other members don't take the law into their own hands and walk right up to Hannes' table to address the headwear issue in person. With each new challenge, he simply smiles, hold up his hand and produces a *Mariachi Martyrs For Christ* pamphlet from his pocket and says, "I think this will explain everything. Read it and get back to me, whenever." Then flicks the back of his left hand in a gesture of obvious dismissal. Leaving each of the confused members stalking off muttering as they read.

A fourth member comes to address the semi-naked Island girls on his jacket and tells him in no uncertain terms he finds the jacket inappropriate dress for the club.

"Do you have any idea what this cost?" demands Hannes in mock anger.

"Nothing I should hope," says his accuser.

"$6,000," he says.

"Bullshit," says the member.

"One of a kind," says Hannes, happily.

"You should be ashamed of yourself!" spits the member.

"Why? Because I bought a Paul Gauguin print jacket at last week's *Women in Pink Charity Auction*? Held right here in this very room for $6,000 even though it's only worth three hundred bucks? In fact, I think I saw you at the cocktail party, what did you buy?"

"Er… we had to leave before the auction, Liz wasn't feeling well." He sputters and scurries off triply embarrassed as his wife is a cancer survivor, involved in the charity and they both know he's too cheap to bid for any of the high ticket auction items.

Hannes leans back in his chair so satisfied he has seen them all off that he pulls out a big stogie and pops it into his mouth without lighting it. He knows smoking is against the club rules anywhere except the patio.

# CHAPTER 3

## SECTION MEETING AND THE FIVE RULES EVERY PRO SHOULD KNOW

S o here I am again at the end of my educational points cycle, short as usual. I call my POS company and have them add a few points for taking training in their system, which of course I never did, but I'm still short. Now I will have to attend the next section educational meeting, which will be more mind-numbing talk about swing plane or another of their endless rules seminars. I check online, fucking rules, don't they get tired of this shit? No one plays by them anyway. Hell, half the PGA Tour players haven't got a clue what they are, and they do this for a living.

How come they never do any seminars on sales? Hello people! That's what we need, more players, not more fucking swing plane concepts or rules! But I smile to myself as I already have a rules question that has stumped everyone I have asked, so that ought to piss someone off!

"I'm playing behind a guy on a tough course with rough so long people were losing their bags. He bangs five balls off the first tee. One short left, two long left, two blocked long right. How long does he get to look for his balls?" No one ever gets this right but the Tour rules official was on the first tee, and I asked him, so I know.

My section requests that everyone shows up for section meetings in a Jacket and tie, so I borrowed Mr. Hannes Loudmouth jacket with the pin-up girls just to spice things up a little. I get a letter three-days later suggesting a less frivolous approach to the next section meeting. What? Me? Frivolous at a PGA rules seminar? I am sworn to uphold the honor and integrity of this ancient game but I sure as hell don't want to be the one giving rules decisions at my club. That's the fastest way I know to create enemies. No sir!

When I get a rules problem at my club. I give them the cell phone number of my old friend and llama breeding expert, Larry Startzel, and let him take the hit for me! After all, he has been the senior official at just about every major event there is, from the US Open to the Ryder Cup. His word is like Charlton Heston's on the mountain or was it Moses, I forget. Anyway, that's a lesson this pro learned a long time ago along with a pink slip from my first head pro job.

**There are five very important rules every PGA pro should know:**

1. You never bet more than $5 with the members
2. You never have more than one drink with the members
3. You never screw the members
4. You never play cards with the members
5. And most importantly of all (since there have been a few variances to rule 3), you do not make rules decisions for your members!

I add the reprimand letter to my files of worthless communication from the PGA in case I ever write a book!

**Amateur Mistake**

There are a number of other unwritten rules that I should probably add that most pros learn the hard way. For example, I make the amateur mistake of playing in Joe Harding's group twice in one month. Now the word is out that that's my "Favorite group." That's where I spend "All my time," and of course they are the group now getting all of the "Preferred tee times." I usually keep a note on my phone to avoid playing with the same group twice in any calendar month, but somehow it happened. I try to kill the rumors by playing with the Ladies nine-hole group, (the longest three hours of my life) and the Tuesday seniors group but the damage has done. I'd have to avoid the Harding group for the rest of the year which is a shame because I really do like those guys. They play fast, pick up after six swats, drink beer while they play, and actually have fun. What a concept!

**Parking Mistake**

The club president pokes his head into my office and asks if I enjoyed my vacation?

"What!" I exclaim in genuine surprise, "I have been here all week. In fact, I haven't even had a day off in two weeks!"

"Oh, it's just your car was not here so naturally, everyone thought you were away on vacation."

"Naturally." I said with no enthusiasm, "It's in the shop I'm driving that red Ford Mustang loner car. Next time I'll ask for a yellow Dodge Charger just like mine, so no one panics."

He smiles in half apology and goes about his business, whatever the fuck that might be. He is a first class dick, and he doesn't like me.

## Rules are Rules

Five minutes later Barney Rubble (not his real name, it's just he's a short, fat blond guy, dumber than a rock, so the name fits) walks behind the counter into my office.

"Jerry, Dr. Walker has brought the same guest seven times, what are you going to do about it?" he asks indignantly.

"Thank him," I offer meekly.

"Thank him? Jerry, you know the rules, a member may only bring the same guest six times in a calendar year." says "Barney" emphatically.

"How do you know he's played seven times?" I quiz.

"Because I have played with them every time he's been here. "

I see, "Did he, by chance, win any money from you?" I ask casually.

"THAT" he spits, "Has nothing to do with it. The man can clearly afford to join the club and should not be playing as a guest."

"I'll mention it to Dr. Walker then."

"Yes, and don't mention my name," says "Barney."

"No of course not you petty, self-righteous prick!" I think, but don't say.

# CHAPTER 4

# THE STRANGE THINGS GOLF DOES TO MEN

The day after the section meeting, a few of us got together and teed it up at my friend Sam's place. After the game, we are sitting around shooting the breeze when someone asks what's the best round you ever shot. Tarchetti starts by recounting his three 59's in local section events blow by blow.

My round takes far less time to recount since it only lasted 30 minutes.

The problem with the best round of my life is that it only lasted four holes and I was 13 only at the time.

For most of my life, I have prided myself on helping people build confidence in their games. Teaching them better ways to get the most from their over-stuffed and aging bodies. Keeping them and my staff motivated. It wasn't always that way, in fact, I must confess to destroying a promising golfing career. This, of course, was not my intention, but where there are winners, there must be losers and the best round of my life certainly changed the life of Tony Whitehouse.

The greatest four holes of my life was a life-changing event for one of our assistant pros.

It was about 10:30 one morning. After hitting my normal 500 range balls, I walked into the pro shop and asked if either of the assistants wanted to play. They worked for a great guy who encouraged them to play golf as long as the shop was being taken care of by one of them. Tony, a burly lad of 17 who had not been playing more than a year and was already a scratch player, jumped off his chair and announced that he was ready to take a buck from me.

On the first hole, a relatively short par four of 335 yards, Tony drove the green and three-putted for par. I hit a driver and wedge to about 10 feet and made birdie. One up.

On the second, Tony once again unleashed a massive drive onto the green. Once again his eagle putt was a little bold and he three-putted. I holed my bunker shot for birdie. Two up.

The third, a difficult uphill par four, Tony unleashed another huge drive, hit wedge to the back of the green and three-putted again. I made an unspectacular par. Three up.

The fourth hole was perhaps the finest hole on the course. The tee was set back some 120 yards into the woods, and you drove over a pond. At about 200 yards, a large pond guarded the left-hand side of the fairway, while a large group of mature pine trees guarded the right. The opening between the pond and the pine trees was no more than twenty-five yards and the fairway sloped directly at the water. The smart play was a two iron, which would leave you short of the pond on the left or the trees on the right if you did not hit it perfectly.

Tony, still mad from three-putting three in a row reached the tee first and was already in motion when I got to the tee. He had hit the finest drive I had ever seen on the hole, threading it between the opening some 280 yards right down the middle. I hit my standard two iron but came off it and pushed it right. It came to rest a few feet short of the pine trees. When I got up to the ball, there was a clear path through the trees. Clear that was if I could hit it through a six-foot gap and keep it straight for twenty more yards.

Tony sarcastically asked me what was I going to do, hole a fairway shot? I replied that was exactly what I had in mind. I took a four iron and hit it perfectly. It raced through the trees, faded slightly as it landed on the green, bounced once, then gently rolled another six feet into the cup for an eagle.

Tony looked at me in disbelief as I jumped up and down. He then turned without a word and marched purposefully towards his ball some 100 yards down the fairway. I hurried after him. Only when he got to his ball he didn't stop, he just stooped down and picked his ball up.

I yelled, "Hey Tony we've got a match!"

He stopped dead for a second, turned and said: "Fuck You!"

With that, he walked the short distance between the fourth green and the pro shop. Handed in his resignation and joined the Marines the following day, thus ending the best round of my life on the fourth hole.

Surprisingly he did not last long in the Marines either, but the Jekyll and Hyde personalities golf brings out in men is amazing.

By the third round of drinks, the conversation has moved on to the funniest thing you ever saw on a golf course.

In the winter, I have the use of a small two-bedroom condo, my grandmother hardly ever uses, at a golf community in Florida where, I am in fact a dues-paying member, winter member (it's cheap) despite the pro's offer to comp me whenever I want to play.

Anyway, a few weeks ago my neighbor Bob drove over in his golf cart and honked his horn outside my home office window. As he yelled, "Can Andrew come out to play?" It was late in the day on a Tuesday and time for a break from my winter paperwork, so I got up from my computer and wandered into the patio closet to get my sticks. A minute or two later we were off towards the first tee as Bob began to tell me what a miserable day he had been having at the office. "East or West?" he said as we got to the clubhouse, "West" I replied.

We went right to the black tees, and after a few casual practice swings, I hit a decent fade down the middle of the fairway. Bob, full of expectation, opened a new sleeve of Titleist's drew out two balls and promptly blasted the first and second right into the bushes. Finding neither, he dropped the remaining ball back in the fairway and promptly launched a five wood even further right. I made four, and we went to the next with Bob muttering all the way.

The second is a very long par four a dogleg left. I nailed one with a little draw down the middle while Bob launched another one right into the bushes. Having found this ball and chipped it out, he launched a three-wood dead right again which sent him back to his bag for another sleeve. This too went right, and we tore off in search of both balls. Finding neither ball, instead of turning the cart back towards the second green, we careened through the trees towards the adjacent eighth tee.

The eighth is a challenging par three of some 220 yards, mainly carry across a picturesque pond with the green guarded front right and left by two large traps. The shot for a good player usually calls for 5-wood but can play longer if the afternoon breeze freshens up.

At 6 pm, the air was still when our cart arrived on the back of the eight tee. Bob took out a new box of Titleist Pro V balls and casually emptied all dozen of them onto the grass. Selecting a five iron from his bag, which was barely enough club to get him to the center of the pond, he proceeded to whack all twelve with wild swings and huge divots flying every which way like a Taz cartoon. To his credit, he swung so hard at one with his right shoulder coming over the ball that it almost made it all the way across the pond the others peppered the water like bugs.

With his arsenal depleted, he jumped back in and drove us both home while I begged him to go back so I could retrieve some of the balls. I guess I still have that anchored feeling from my childhood of how great it felt to find a new Pro Trajectory Titleist.

Exactly a week later Bob's cart was in the driveway again. He made some cute comment like he always did and I went to the garage to get my clubs. This time we started out on the eighth tee of the East course. It was uneventful. Then we came to the ninth a long par-five that doglegs around a large lake and heads straight uphill to the clubhouse. The lake cannot be carried from the back tees, at least not by mere club pros like me, and so the ball must be aimed left. I hit my usual safe shot, and Bob rifled off what looked like a winner at first but gently faded until it found the edge of the lake.

The ball was clearly visible in the shallow water sitting on white sand, some ten or twelve feet from shore. At first, Bob tried to without success to retrieve it with his club. Then he took the rake from his cart, that almost worked. Finally, after laboriously trying to stretch his arm another agonizing inch, he threw down the rake down and wadded into the lake to retrieve his prized possession. I just sat in the cart and howled with laughter. One week ago the frustrated golfer hit fifty dollars' worth of balls into the middle of the lake on purpose, the next he risks, snakes, alligators and quicksand to save a single pill!

There have been more tragic events, like the pro I played with in the section pro one year who shot 36-54, calmly sign his card and thanked his playing partners only to blow his brains out in the parking lot with a Colt 45. Not that we haven't all felt like that but once or twice, but actually doing it… it's a strange thing what golf does to men!

# CHAPTER 5

## Why I Hate The Golf Channel

I hate the Golf Channel, hate it, hate it, hate it with a passion. Not because I don't like watching their tournament golf or even some of the shows, I hate it because whatever teaching pro was on last night will show up at my range first thing the next day having hijacked one of my member's brains.

**For example Sid Nichols today:**

"Jerry, I was watching TV last night, and they were discussing something called the X-factor. What is it?" He asks.

"An English TV show like American Idol, I think?" I say, pretending to know nothing of which he speaks.

"No, no," Sid insists, "I was watching The Golf Channel. There was a famous golf instructor, Jim something?"

"Mclean," I offer.

"Yes, I think so, blonde guy. He was talking about the X-factor swing."

"Sid," I say emphatically, "We need to work on some other factors first. You've got at least 23 more letters to go before we need to worry about that X."

"Really," he insists, "It was very interesting…"

"I am sure it was, he's a great teacher, but he's not out here on the range with you, I am. I think there are a number of areas we have to address first, like the way you grip the club as though you are trying to choke a rattlesnake, the fact you aim 30 yards right of your target and that your clubface averages seven degrees closed at impact." I say, but experience tells me my rational approach to game improvement will be rejected. Sadly, I am right!

"Yes, yes I know all that, you've told before, but I'd like to try this X-factor stuff just to see if it works…"

(A sigh with an eye roll) "Ok you warm up, I'm going to grab a couple of swing aids."

I go back to the office flick through a copy of Jim's book just to be sure my X-factor sounds like his X-factor and return with a couple of props. X-factor day it is…

Next comes Peter Hargreaves, he's just seen Ledbetter on the Golf Channel. He bought his book, and he's wearing his signature hat. He wants to know all about the A-swing. Forget the fact he hardly gets the club much beyond his hips, that he's at least 60 pounds overweight and seventy plus years old! This old dog doesn't want training; he wants some new tricks and today's will be the A-swing. Luckily, I also have a copy of that in my library.

I have a simple philosophy that serves me well on the lesson tee; I try diligently twice to get my students to do the right thing, then I just do whatever they ask.

A day later, Sandy Collins is walking towards me with what looks like a vintage Golf Digest in her hands. "Jerry I have been reading this very interesting piece by a famous teacher called, Jim Flick, about the L – L drill. "

**A**-swing, **X**-factor **L** –drill, It's like a fucking nightmare episode of *Sesame Street* out here on the range.

"I don't think he recommends that drill anymore," I remark.

"Oh," says Sandy, "Why?"

"Because he's dead," I say flatly.

She looks at me horrified and then smiles, "You are just having a little fun with me aren't you?"

I open my hands in mock surrender, "OK, let's take a look at it," and put my hand out for the magazine so I can pretend to read the article. On the plus side, the five minutes it takes to read the four-page spread is five fewer minutes I have to look at her abomination of a golf swing!

It's not just the Golf Channel either; it could be a Miller or Faldo making a casual comment about a Tour Player's swing that a member latches onto and runs with like a rabid dog. It could be a blog post, Golf Magazine or my latest and great nemesis YOUTUBE. To get on the Golf Channel, you need to at least have a clue. There is no such filter on YouTube. Any Tom, Dick or Harry with a smartphone can claim to be a golf pro and post whatever garbage they like about the golf swing. It's like the 26-handicap guy at the range teaching the 40-handicap guy how to play golf and blasting that "knowledge" worldwide.

There is a second reason I hate the Golf Channel. It is because every other student I teach shows up with a $150 contraption designed to increase their swing speed, promote a good takeaway, smooth out their tempo, line up their fifth putt or some other such nonsense.

Golf has every other sport beat when it comes to the variety of weird and wonderful gadgets, dubious and otherwise, to help improve your game. There are thousands of contraptions, many of which would not look out of place in the medieval torture chamber I once visited in Spain. They are designed to help you keep your head down, break your wrist in the right place, keep your arms connected and ensure everything stays on plane. I even had a guy once who had something connected to his balls and almost castrated himself!

If you're like my members, instead of taking a bathroom break, you stay rooted to the couch to watch those Golf Channel infomercials that promise to help you groove your swing or add 20 yards to your drives.

Who can forget the Alien wedge? The Perfect Club? Or the Sensei grip? A boat paddle-like attachment that none other than Jack Nicklaus referred to as "The most practical training aid he has ever seen." No doubt largely because he was getting paid a large amount of money to say so.

The truth is that while many training aids are over-hyped, some really can help you improve your tempo, your alignment, and your game. I have tried a few including the Medicus, the famed double-hinged club that has enjoyed a longer success run on late night TV than David Letterman. It really does a good job of slowing down your swing and helping you with tempo.

I have also used a straightjacket promoted a long time ago by Jimmy Ballard to help me "stay connected." While as a kid, I had a golf ball with just a tiny strip of rubber to promote pure striking of a putt. If not hit perfectly square it would wobble like a drunk. It was a very good one, and I used to practice with it on the tiled floor of my hallway so I'd be ready for the speed when I eventually reached, those glass-like greens at Augusta National. Sigh…

Instead of all the nonsense and gimmicks, I try to blind my students with pure science using my TrackMan to show the scientific evidence of the golf swing.

For instance, that it's actually possible to hit the ball dead left by coming severely into out with the club face dead shut. While my students still insist they "Must have come over it!" if the ball went left. They say that the golf ball never lies, but golfers do. Mainly to themselves.

Let's not forget the bookworms with hundreds of books on swing theories in their personal libraries, the type that come to their lessons clutching their prized information with the pages dog-eared and the key paragraphs highlighted in yellow pen.

**I'll comment on just a few:**

**Golf My Way** – I have the highest respect for Jack, but this book ruined more golf careers in the 70's and 80's than any book every written before or since. Including mine! "Pick the ball off the turf," he wrote, "While taking divots the size of Manhattan." I shake my head that I never saw the chasm between what he wrote and what he actually did, I was just young and stupid I guess.

**The Five Modern Fundamentals of Golf** – Modern once, somewhere around 1950!

**The Short Game Bible** – Written by the world's highest-paid golf coach who can't actually break 90, never won a tournament and isn't actually a golf pro. Go figure, one of the best-selling golf books ever.

**Bobby Jones on Golf** – A great book because the first half is biographical and a treat to read. The second half, the instruction part, I highly recommend to all my students who play in hickory events, for those of you who prefer graphite and steel... em... not so useful.

Of course, that doesn't stop the likes of Mick Walton bringing a copy of the book to every lesson where he is keen to point out the differences between my swing thoughts and those of "The great Bobby Jones." Imagine what he could have done with an Epic Driver and a Pro V1, the guy might have won something!

Meanwhile, I am working on my own book, swing aid and video series called, **Shanking for Distance!**

# CHAPTER 6

# ON THE RANGE WITH THE BLACK WIDOW!

As golf professionals, it's not unusual to have the bored housewives, trophy wives and girlfriends we teach flirt with us a little. Even the old grannies get a gleam in their misty eyes every now and then and try to get a little smile or rise out of us with an out of character comment about what they might do if only they were a little younger.

Mrs. Green (Samantha) was different; she was a full-on nymphomaniac. She was sixty-something, although she insisted she was ten years younger. Truth is she was still pretty good looking albeit with the help of numerous top surgeons in LA and Miami, plus a personal fitness coach six days a week. She modeled herself on a seventies version of Dolly Parton. She had colorful clothes, big hair, and even bigger tits. Tits that she mentioned in casual conversation by various pet names at every opportunity. Did you know there are over one hundred slang words for breasts? She knew them all!

Two of her four husbands had died. The other two she had divorced, leaving some in the club to refer to her as the "Black widow." Still, their estates had made her wealthy. She drove a baby blue Ferrari California that always pulled into the club with the top down and "Jolene" or Dolly's version of "I Will Always Love You (far better than Whitney's she would always say)," blasting from the stereo.

She played golf and tennis at the club on alternate days. She was hopeless at both but took lessons twice a week from the Tennis Pro, Brad and me. She liked me better because although Brad was younger and far better looking, he was gay. So, while she "adored him" she knew her flirting was always going to be in vain. With me, apparently, she thought hope sprang eternal despite my steely resolve NOT to get involved with members or their girlfriends.

Every lesson for her was an exercise in getting me to touch her body to illustrate a swing point or respond to a question about the role her "massive mambas" played in her golf swing.

"Jerry, do you think there's something I can do with my boobies to help me hit the ball father?"

"Do you think if I wore a tighter sports bra to hold in my melons it would give me more room to attack the ball?"

"What's the best way to get my hooters involved in the swing?"

"What should I do with my knockers when I turn my shoulders?"

I looked at her dumbfounded although I should have guessed.

Seeing my confusion, she practically yelled "Knockers! That's what they call boobs in England. "

"Oh," I say, "Do they?"

"They most certainly do!" she said emphatically.

"I really wish I didn't have such huge Jugs!"

Well in that case maybe you should have just asked for extra-large and not supersized I thought to myself.

At first, it was very embarrassing, especially when other members were within earshot. But after a while, like most things in this business, you just take it in stride.

The constant requests to put her in position were another thing. She loved being touched. "I am very kinesthetic," she announced, "I cannot learn by watching, you must move me into the positions you want me to achieve."

I had already moved all the way to the far end of the range as a matter of policy. We were working on shoulder turn, and I had my hand pushing her left shoulder gently, she moved quickly and it slipped onto her left breast. I snatched it back with a look of horror like I had placed it on a hot stove.

"Jerry," she said sternly in mock aristocratic tone, "They don't bite!"

Funny, I'd been to two PGA seminars on sexual harassment, but they never addressed what to do when the members were harassing me. They just assumed it would be me harassing the member. WTF!

She would end every lesson with her golf joke of the day, most of which I could do no better than a forced smile and internal eye roll.

**For example, this was Monday's effort.**

"Jerry, you'll love this one…"

An elderly couple are playing together in the annual golf club couples championship. The game has ended up in a playoff hole, and everything rides on an 8-inch putt that the wife must make. Aware of how critical this final putt is, she takes her stance, and her husband can see her trembling.

Well, the wife putts, the ball sails clear past the hole, and the couple lose the match. On the way home in the car, it's obvious from the atmosphere that her husband is not happy, in fact, he is fuming.

"I cannot believe that you missed that simple putt!" he said to his wife. "That putt was no longer than my dick."

The wife just looked over at her husband, smiled and said, "Yes dear, but it was much harder!"

**This was Wednesday's**

Sometimes a man can get his way without it costing a small fortune...

Three friends always wanted to play golf on a Saturday afternoon, but it was made almost impossible by the demands of their wives.

One day, after many failed attempts, they finally got together on the golf course and were waiting at the first tee when the first friend said, "I had to buy my wife a diamond necklace to get to play today!"

The second followed, "That's nothing, I had to buy MY wife a new sports car to get out here today!"

The third said, "Boy you guys are a couple of wimps; I didn't have to buy my wife anything at all!"

The others just looked at him in amazement, and asked how he managed that!

The smartest of the three said, "It was easy. When I got up this morning I looked her straight in the eye and asked, 'Golf course or intercourse?'"

She threw me a sweater and said, "Take this, it might get chilly out there!"

There was one thing very consistent about her jokes they always had sexual innuendos. It was like she was some sex-starved nymphomaniac, she just never stopped talking about sex and she never stopped hitting on me.

"Jerry, you should join me for dinner sometime, I'm free this weekend."

"Sorry, playing in an event up-state."

"Jerry there's a party at the yacht club Friday night."

"Sounds wonderful. Unfortunately, I already accepted dinner with the Smiths."

"Would you like to play in the Pebble Beach Pro-Am with me?"

"That would be delightful, but I think your handicap is about 30 strokes over their limit."

Couldn't she just go on Cougar.com like the rest of her generation and leave me alone?

Apparently not.

Finally, after several weeks, she wore me down.

"Jerry I've just installed a new putting green at my house, I'd like to get your opinion on it and I'll take a putting lesson while you are here. Can we change my Friday lesson to 5 pm at my home instead of the range, you said it was your last of the day?"

I had run out of excuses it was either tell her and her $250 a week plus gifts to get lost and deal with whatever political ramifications or rumors she might start, or capitulate. I chose capitulation. What the heck, it was the weekend and although she was a pain in the ass as member, a lousy student and a little past her sell-by date she was at least fun!

When I get there, the house is huge, the pool is huge, the cabana is huge. Blondie's "Call Me," the theme from the movie *American Gigolo* with Richard Gere, is blasting from the outdoor speakers. As if I needed one, it was another sign how this might end.

I don't remember much.

We spent half an hour on the new putting green with her encouraging me to place my hands in various place I had tried hard to avoid on the range. My protests didn't last too long, after all, there was no one to see us and her legs were still very attractive in her short skirt.

Next, she made us both an amazing Mojito. It was a very hot day, and the first one went to straight my head. By the third, we were both naked in the huge pool with me looking admiringly at her built-in floatation devices that seem to have a life of their own as I licked them gently. It ended in the hot tub with her Botox-infused lips wrapped tightly around my Johnson (us guys have lots of slang words for our parts too). I woke the next day in a world of alcohol-infused hurt in the bedroom of the poolside cabana.

She was nowhere to be seen, but there was a covered tray outside the door with a bagel, fruit, juice and a jug of coffee. I eat the bagel greedily trying to get something in me to soak up the rum. There was a note too written in red pen in a flowery female script.

"What fun. I loved the way you kept your head down. Looking forward to my next lesson. Love, Sam."

It was fun, I think. At least what I could remember of it was fun, but this could only end badly, very badly. Which is why I am eternally grateful to Fabio, her 29-year old Argentinian fitness instructor, who in a fit of Latin passion ran off to Cabo to marry her a week later. I only hope for his sake he gets his green card before it all goes south (he had long overstayed his visa), and for her sake I hope she had a prenup. I'm sure she must of, she's had plenty of practice.

For now at least golf and golf pros are off her agenda!

# CHAPTER 7

# THE NEVER-ENDING
# CHALLENGE OF THE GAME

I t took me a decade as a pro to get comfortable just reading out the rules before a shotgun or the winners of each event at the end. As I gained confidence and realized that the audience was usually half in the bag and couldn't care less about me making a gaff or a fool of myself, I started to relax. I started considering some courses on after-dinner speaking, and I have to say I polished up my act to the point where my members and fellow pros started to take notice. An anecdote here, a joke there, a small poke at someone I knew would not be offended, and my reputation started to grow.

The club decided to put on a "Ted Talk" kind of night about the different aspects of the wonderful game of golf and asked four people, including me, to put together a presentation. Since each of us would be paid

$750 and I thought it might enhance my reputation at the club, I said "Sure." Funny how time changes things, I would have ran and hid a few years ago at the very thought of speaking to a room full of people.

There is a full house when I get up to give my speech, and it's already getting a little rowdy. But they calm down as start my slideshow and I take the mic to deliver my speech...

## The Never-Ending Challenge of the Game

Is it not Murphy's Law that the day you drive well, your iron shots are poor, or the day you hit all the greens, your putter is as cold as ice? With golf, every day is a fresh start on your never-ending quest to shoot a lower score, par a specific hole or hit a certain type of shot well.

The initial challenge for the beginner is, of course, to get the ball airborne. Hitting it straighter comes next and then further. Getting the ball to stop more or less where you want it to is hugely satisfying and worth all the effort required. Finally, there's the rather important business of actually persuading the ball to drop into the small hole.

Then there are those awkward tasks such as splashing out of bunkers or chipping off a variety of lies. As you grow more proficient, you will be introduced to the fiendishly tricky business of shaping a shot and become acquainted with the hook, slice, draw, fade, high and low ball.

Then there are lies, damned lies and, most difficult of all, downhill lies. To make things even trickier, there are all manner of surfaces from springy links turf to lush country club, from woodland to desert and the threadbare fairways of the local municipal to the manicured heaven that is Augusta National.

And let's not forget the mental aspect of the game. Do you, for example, go through an identical pre-shot routine before you strike the ball? Do you visualize the shot, fist pump when you hole a putt and are you always positive about your game?

While mastering the techniques and literally getting to grips with the golf, you must also understand the etiquette, which can be every bit as fraught and problematic as where you place your right thumb on the shaft of the club. However, much more important than understanding how to swing a club is knowing how to score! To this end, you must examine your strategy for playing each hole and consider employing different clubs from the tee to enhance the chances of achieving success.

Okay, now you are finally ready to sit down with a six-pack of beer and study the 45-page 'Rules of Golf' which you have had in your bag ever since you took up golf five years ago but have never bothered to open. If you do read it, you will have a considerable edge over your opponents who won't ever have bothered.

All the above might seem like a lot of trouble to go through just to enjoy what is in effect a pleasant stroll in the park. But I assure you, my friends, it is not. Golf is a never-ending challenge that has to be embraced mentally, physically and emotionally for the better of all mankind!

There is simply no sport that can challenge you in so many ways and offers the opportunity for so many personal victories even when you lose. Whatever the final outcome, your longest drive, best putt, holed bunker shot, magnificent recovery or hearing that satisfying click when you make perfect contact will induce a lingering smile as you walk down the fairway.

There is a long applause when I finish, and I feel deeply satisfied that I just made $750 bucks in twenty minutes rather than standing in the heat of the lesson tee for six hours! I must look into doing more of this, it's an interesting sideline.

# CHAPTER 8

## HOMEOWNERS ASSOCIATION ARMAGEDDON

Now, being a golf pro, you would think I have nothing whatsoever to do with the Homeowners Association, and you'd be right, I have absolutely nothing to do with it. Which does not for one moment deter any of the members using me as their first point of call whenever they do anything to upset anyone!

They come into the pro shop waving letters and exclaiming:

"Jerry, what can be done about this?"

"Jerry, what can WE (emphasis on WE) do about this?" "WE can't do anything because I have nothing to do with the Homeowners Association," I plead as I open my hands in helpless surrender.

"But Jerry you're the pro!" they insist.

I sigh and look at whatever letter they are waiving before mutter some worthless advice on what to do next. Like, "Call Bill Thomas he's a lawyer, or I think Fred Durkins had a similar issue, why don't you see what he did?"

"Right," they say and march off in search of new comrades.

There was one time I did intervene on behalf of an anonymous member with a petulance for loud jackets. This was only to protect the club from further suffering after his previous campaign against the Homeowners Association had brought the club an Armageddon of heartache for four long weeks. Four of the funniest weeks of my life, to be sure, but I didn't want it repeating, which was exactly what he was planning to do if they didn't back off on his dogs!

It all started with a typical HOA form letter that stated:

> During a routine inspection of your property, it was found you had constructed an illegal dog pen on your property and it should be removed at once.

Mr. Hannes responded with his own letter asking how, if he indeed had a dog pen which was clearly not visible from the street, would it be possible for anyone to know he had one without trespassing?

He was told the HOA had the right to inspect his property.

After six unreturned calls to the property management company (later proved by his cell phone records) and two emails, he was served with a lawsuit from the HOA for lack of ANY response to their demands.

He then sent them this letter:

TO: The HOA

RE: The Practically (If you are not trespassing) Invisible Dog Pen

From: Mr. Hannes

**Dear Fellow Members, Residents and Board Members:**

The pool area on my house is large and raised up high above the ground, giving our three dogs (one's on the way out) a great view of the passing golfers.

The guy across the street, whose house you can see, complained numerous times that the dogs were barking and that they keep getting out (by biting through the screen). This happened numerous times.

Although I would not say that the dogs are barkers, it annoyed this guy enough that it became a problem and he called up very heated one day shortly after accosting me while I was playing.

My wife became very upset and said she would fix the problem at once.

I went out of town, and when I came back, there was the dog pen. The dogs can't see the players, and they can't get out and bother people.

Now, I do realize she should have asked permission, but that would have taken time, and the situation would have got out of hand.

So she did what she thought best and solved the problem at once to appease the neighbors.

*View of offending pen from the edge of my property line the closest, you can get from the course.*

*View of offending pen from <u>six-feet</u> away, notice the fast-growing evergreen bushes!*

The truth of the matter is if you are not  ON MY PROPERTY, a few feet away, it is in fact invisible. To take any picture where you can actually see the fence would involve trespassing on my property or a seriously large zoom lens.

Remember the fairway is thirty yards right of where those pictures were taken. When the bushes grow, no one will know it exists.

Now how did we get to the stage where I get sued? I mean, that's all we need in this community is more lawsuits!

Did I ignore the letters?

No, on the contrary, I attempted to contact Trixie Monaco the very day I got the first letter in October. I sent her an email and left a voicemail. Two weeks later, I sent another email and left another voicemail. In all, I left six messages for her including a detailed one two weeks ago, taken by Sandy. She never called back until today when I had my entire staff call Melrose until she did!

She told me she had got no calls or e-mails from me. I do of course have cell phone bills which will prove I called numerous times.

None the less, due to her lack of response I was served a lawsuit.

Now what do we do from here:

A)  I can obviously remove the offending "invisible pen," BUT IF I do the dogs will go right back to the pool area. They will bark at any golfer who comes close to my property, and they will no doubt chew through the screens and roam the neighborhood again. At will.

The guy across the fairway will get pissed off and as I mentioned he has already accosted me once while playing. Stepping in front of my cart and refusing to move until he told me how upset he was with my dogs getting out!

B)  I could have the dogs put down, which would save me a good deal of trouble, but is unlikely to be a popular move with my wife and kids.

C)  I could fight the lawsuit, perhaps dream up one of my own (seems like a popular pastime at here for many residents). But I am busy and going to

Europe for the entire summer, so any fight would have to wait until I get back.

D) You could stand by the rulebook (I won't even start on how many exceptions exist at this point. Ok, I'll share one. Last year I was asked to remove a basketball hoop from my yard that was put in over ten years ago, long before I bought the property. I did as asked even through there are five other such hoops in the community including one on the same street that still stands!) You obviously can tell me to take down the "Invisible, problem-solving pen" and accept the OTHER community problems that it creates detailed in Option A.

E) We could agree that my wife should have asked for permission, she will retroactively do so. You will approve it, and we will take whatever additional steps are necessary to hide the offending pen (totally) from the naked eye. The dogs won't get out to roam the neighborhood, they will bark far less since they can't see much from the pen, the guy across the street won't get pissed, and we all live happily ever after.

Obviously, a community has to have rules but is obvious also that it should amend those rules for the good of the community. Given the circumstances, my wife solved the problem quickly and painlessly. I hope you will be so good as to do the same by choosing Option E and removing the suit at once!

Thanking You In Advance Your Cooperation,
*Mark Hannes, Shella, Fleagel and Lexi*

Unfortunately, for the Homeowners Association and the golf club they did not give him any cooperation. His wife removed the dog pen, he was fined $1,785, and he left for the summer in Europe.

Two weeks later, fifty or so homeowners received a formal letter looking like it was from the HOA signed with a similar name and cc'd to both the developer and developers law firm.

All the letters started in the same way:

**Homeowners Association**

Dear Name:

**During a routine inspection of your property, it was found that:**

And, finished in the same way, "Please attend to this matter at once to avoid further actions including fines."

Trixie Monaco

Property manager

CC: Sid Peters

CC: James and Howe Esq.

In between were snippets of Machiavellian genius aimed to inflict maximum conflict and divine retribution.

For example, an Indian doctor with a large rust stain on his driveway from his sprinkler water was told.

**During a routine inspection of your property, it was found that:**

That there was a large curry stain on your driveway and it should be removed at once.

A home with a beautiful garden of flowers was told that three of the species were not approved by the HOA and should be removed at once.

His neighbors on either side were sent a picture of his beautiful garden and told they should be embarrassed at the average state of their garden in a world-class community and should up their game to make their gardens look like their neighbor's.

A small house with a large American Flag was told that the flag was too large for the size of his house and that, while his patriotism was admired, he should get a smaller flag or upgrade to a larger house.

A home with a bust of the Virgin Mary in her garden was told to remove the figure or risk upsetting her Muslim neighbors.

One homeowner was told to remove a chimney as it was the only one on that row of homes and it looked sorely out of place.

And so it went on…

According to emails flying around the club, it was going to cost $33,000 to remove it. The dumb bitch actually got a quote!

As did the Korean doctor who was told he had built his wall too close to the course and had move his wall back three feet.

The emails started flying. Lawyers started calling. Threatening letters were sent, and the property management company and club were besieged with angry phone calls while having no idea what was going on.

No one caught on it was a ruse because each of the letters had one snippet of truth that spoke personally to each homeowner that set the wheels in monition.

The result was the almost total paralysis of the development for nearly four weeks. Even after that, people who were out of town when the letter first hit were still calling. The police were called, but no crime had been committed. It was just a big joke, but only one person was laughing!

Funny thing was two people were suspected of being the perpetrators of the campaign, an old New York lawyer and member who did nothing to dispel the notion and a recently fired LPGA pro who was a club employee, batting for the other team and sought unfair dismissal. I thought I knew, who the real perpetrator was but since he had been in Europe for over three weeks no one even considered Mr. Hannes.

**The upside according to him:**

The lying bitch at the property management company resigned and they were fired a week later for their handling of the matter.

It should have ended there, except for one rouge squirrel a year later.

The offending squirrel chewed through the screen on top of the pool and fell into the pool splashing around for hours. His (now) two dogs were going ballistic. The neighbors, rather than being neighborly, and checking what in the hell was going on called the Pro shop, who called the guard gate, who called the manager, the HOA, and CNN for all I know! When Mr. Hannes got home, the dogs were put in the house, the half-drowned squirrel retrieved with a net and the barking stopped at once.

The HOA immediately fired off a letter and the threat of hefty fines. Hannes immediately fired back a response pointing out none of this would have happened had they let him keep the dog pen as he requested in the first place and explained the situation re the squirrel. The HOA said that immediate measures must be taken or he would be hit with a $300 fine.

I did not wait for his response but instead went to see the developer's secretary with an anonymous message.

The message was the following:

"If you thought Operation Banshee caused problems wait until you see what happens with Operation Nemesis!"

"I am not sure I know what this means, Jerry." She said. "I think I do," I told her. She caught on at once when I mentioned the previous campaign and its month-long fall out of lawsuits, emails and accusations The recriminations of which were still being felt at the club and in the community.

Thankfully she had the good senses to send Mr. Hannes a letter thanking him for addressing the matter, when in fact he had done no such thing.

They simply don't pay me enough for this type of work!

# CHAPTER 9

## ROAD TRIPPING

B ack in the day, I got a dozen free balls every month, a new pro bag every year and clubs whenever I asked. I could play golf almost anywhere for free with a call to the host pro and bring a guest. Now they even charge me at the PGA golf courses!

One of the benefits of being a golf pro that still exists is the opportunity to take free golf trips. Now, the downside of this is you have to take between three and eleven members with you depending on the location to get travel free. But, if you choose wisely and get the word out quickly and quietly you can usually fill it up with the "right' members before everyone hears about it and you find yourself on vacation with some life-draining zombies.

Every trip has its story. The story is never the same but usually involves some or all of these ingredients: girls, booze, cops, injuries, a rules incident and at least one unbelievable shot which would always fall into the best or worst shot we had ever seen category.

For a decade we had a trip to Carmel, California. The first year two of the guys fell off a bed wrestling each other. The result being one broken arm and one dislocated shoulder which was a shame as it was the first night of a five day trip to Pebble Beach.

Year five or six, I forget which, was the only year I remember without causalities. Myself, Mr. Hannes, Mr. Lynch and Mr. Blaney had come back from off-property at about 11:30 pm without incident. The rest of the group had opted to stay in-house for the seafood buffet. As we returned, there were a ton of cars leaving a big gala charity event. We walked into the bar at Spanish Bay where Dana our favorite bartender and part-time real estate agent was ready for us and greeted us warmly.

There was one guy sitting at the end of the bar in a cowboy hat, other than that the bar was deserted. We ordered drinks and took four stools at the bar all chatting with Dana. After a while, Blaney glances at the man several stools down and stares at him. He nudges me, "Hey is that Garth Brooks he whispers?" I look and tell him I have no idea not only is it dim in the bar, but I also don't have my glasses and I have no idea what Garth Brooks looks like anyway. I nudge Lynch, "Hey Lynch Mob is that Garth Brooks?"

He looks, he shrugs, "I don't know could be." Hannes never one to be shy asks what the hell we are whispering about. "We were wondering if the guy at the end of the bar is Garth Brooks." Whispers Lynch.

Hannes, of course, has no shame, so he just yells, down the bar, "Hey Buddy, are you Garth Brooks?"

He looks up "Yea," he nods and goes back to looking at his drink (this was before iPhones, people used to do that for entertainment). I am dreading what's next, but I know it's coming.

"Well, sing us a song!" Roars Hannes.

Garth Brooks turns to Hannes and says "I came here to do a charity gig and I'm not sure you can afford a song."

Challenge his manhood, challenge his intelligence, call him the son of a bitch but you do not challenge his ability to buy whatever the hell he wants!

"What did the last song go for?" Lynch asks casually.

"Ten grand," said Brooks in a matter of fact tone.

We all smile because we all know what's coming next. Hannes removes his fanny pack in which he always keeps… you guessed it ten grand in cash and slides it down the bar, like a challenge in an old cowboy movie. Brooks stops it with his left hand before it plows into his drink and knocks it off the bar.

No one speaks, no one moves. There is real tension in the air.

Brooks scratches under his nose with his index finger, unzips the bag holds it opens for a second to check the contents and with an aw-shucks grin says "Ok, it's for a good cause, I'll be back."

After ten minutes, we thought he'd just left with the ten grand, but sure enough, he returned with a guitar, sat down in a chair by the fireplace and played not one but three songs to an audience of four. Five if you count Dana who was practically wetting herself with excitement. Then he simply got up nodded and left, the room. You simply can't make this shit up.

The following year the lead car in our three-car group was pulled over by Police on 17-mile Drive as our 18-year-old rookie threw up out the window. This ended with our driver in jail on a DUI charge. A charge he eventually beat seven years and $50,000 later. Which only goes to prove you can buy justice!

Three years later we had long since wised up and took the Spanish Bay shuttle off property instead. This year, however, resulted in a mutiny of the already inebriated passengers when after progressing seven or eight miles down 17-mile Drive the driver was called back to pick up another passenger at the Lodge. After failing to bribe him not to return, one of the group staged a heart attack. The bus stopped, and we helped him down. Once at the side of the road Mr. Hannes already quite toasty casually pushed the driver down a steep grass embankment and threw a couple of hundred dollar bills his way with assurances we'd be back in a couple of hours. Then we simple high-jacked the bus. I forget who drove, but it wasn't me or Hannes.

We did have the sense to change restaurants, but the cops showed up as we ordered dessert anyway. All 12 of us were detained for several hours but were released without charges when Pebble agreed to forget the incident if we agreed never to return. Good job it was our last night, it was too fucking expensive anyway!

Last year I hit Cabo, the Dominican Republic, Florida, and Scotland. This year, I'm over here in the Emerald Isle, sitting in the clubhouse at Old Head, in the very seat (so I'm told) that Tiger sat in not a week ago. A pint of Harp Lager is already on its way to my table as I listen to the strange chatter emanating from the table behind me, in a language I don't understand (it turned out the guys were from Shreveport).

Looking out of the window, the lighthouse stands on a massive cliff overlooking the 17th green, that despite being almost 600-yards from the tee, I had hit in two earlier. Thanks to what my caddie, Des, referred to as "a slight helping breeze." (In Florida, we give breezes like that their own names!)

Des, a scrawny man of indeterminate vintage and dressed in pre-war tweed, is already propping up the bar. There he is loudly recounting to anyone who will listen that "His Man" - that being me - had hit the 17th this very afternoon with two shots *"The likes of which he had never seen!"* Thus ensuring my continued patronage in picking up the tab for his entire evening's consumption!

The next day we arrive at Waterville after a hair-raising three-hour drive down roads no bigger than bobsled runs. Each turn a minefield of cows, sheep, tractors and on-coming cars apparently oblivious to the fact there was not possibly room for two cars to share the road. A fact that did nothing to stop their oncoming velocity as we dove into hedge after hedge.

We take the obligatory photo of the group standing by the Payne Stewart statute on the range and tee it up in the drizzle. On the 12th I stood just three over and had hit a particularly good drive downwind on the par five. Since the 12th sits up above the front nine, the caddie took pains in pointing out that everyone on the front was now heading for the clubhouse like a herd of sheep ahead of the oncoming deluge.

I stated I was going to hit the green in two and make birdie.

He replied, "You're a little tapped in the head mister." Which, I assume meant he was questioning my sanity.

I did indeed make birdie on 12 leaving me just two over with six to play on this venerable links course. Unfortunately, the wind and rain hit us on the 13th tee and the lowest score I had coming back into the wind was 9, on a par three, where I hit driver, 9 iron. Sometimes you really should listen to your caddie, even if he is Irish!

We spent the night in the lovely town of Killarney. It was a little past midnight when we left the last of the five pubs we had visited. It was by far the best of the bunch with live Irish music putting everyone in a festive mood.

We came around yet another blind corner to be met some 100 yards down the road by a car parked sideways headlights shining across the road and a man in black standing in the middle with a torch. The flashing blue lights on the car, parked in the gates to a field gave away his identity.

Harry grabs for the breath mints and pulls slowly to a stop. He fumbles for the window switch on the unfamiliar rental car and keeps the cop waiting several seconds before he finds it.

The cop peers in and shines the torch on each us, while uttering a pleasant "Good evening gentlemen" to the group, in a thick Irish accent. Pulling his head out of the car he peers down at Harry and casually asks, "Have you been drinking Sir?"

"What makes you say that officer?" Says Harry, calmly while surely knowing he's already fucked.

No field sobriety test here, walking toe to toe down straight lines, the roads don't stay straight long enough to use that one. Here, it's blow into the bag and see what the mighty breathalyzer crystals have to say.

GUILTY

or

NOT GUILTY

I was not really sure what the limit was but was pretty sure it was somewhere south of the five or six pints Harry had consumed, perhaps a long way south.

"Why do I think you might have been drinking sir? Says the officer pleasantly, "Well, for a start you are driving on the wrong side of the road."

"How the hell can you tell? The damn roads here are so small both the mirrors are practically touching the hedge on either side." Says Harry defiantly.

"Where are you going?" asks the cop

"Back to our hotel?" Says Harry

"Which is?" asks the cop patiently.

"The big one on the lake!"

"The big one on the Lake," the cop repeats slowly.

"American golfers are you?"

"How'd you guess?" says Carl from the back seat without actually meaning to say it out loud.

"Oh," says the cop sarcastically, "I'm training to be a detective."

Someone stifled a laugh and for a few seconds no one spoke, then to our surprise, he said, "Ok, follow me, slowly, and keep your windows down."

He walks back to his car while we all look at each other and shrug. We drive the two miles behind the police car with his lights flashing back to the lodge on the lake.

We get out of the car and the cop is standing there holding up an envelope. On it in large black letters where written the words **Mulchay's Boys Home**.

"Gentlemen, before you go in, may I ask if you would be willing to make a donation. I want to be clear you are under no obligation to make a donation, as I am under no obligation to offer you a breathalyzer test at this time. But I would also like to point out that it's Friday night which means anyone taken in for DUI will not see a judge until Monday morning, most likely Monday afternoon, it's a busy day you know. Furthermore, it's going to cost you a couple of thousand quid before you are done.

"Is this a shakedown?" I ask incredulously.

"It most certainly is not," he says in a very offended tone, "Everyone except the driver is free to go about their business. But I think we all know what the situation here is boys?"

We all dug into our pockets and came up with about two hundred pounds between us. He made a face like he was not that impressed but took the cash and stuffed it into the envelope. He then walked with us into the hotel and handed the envelope to the desk clerk with a one Euro coin and instructions to mail it. Which the clerk did at once by placing a stamp on it dropping it in an adjacent mailbox on the wall.

"Good night gents, thank you for that it, makes a big difference to the boys," said the cop and with a mock salute he turned and left.

"Well at least it was for a good cause," I say to no one in particular, but saw the desk clerk nod solemnly in agreement. We went to the bar for a nightcap and charged it to the room since no one had any cash left. We would have to hit an ATM in the morning, the caddies here still don't take Amex in return for a loop.

After a quick trip into town for cash, we played 18 on the beautiful parkland course and headed back towards Cork. We were already a couple of miles outside of town on a narrow winding road when we went over a hump back bridge, and passed a small grey stone building on the banks of a stream.

"Stop!" I yelled, but the car went another hundred yards before coming to a standstill

"Back up."

"What?"

"Back up!"

He did so slowly until we were outside a small pub

"The son of a bitch!" I cried.

Everyone else saw the pub's name at the same time as they saw the A-frame sign that offered: Adult babysitting free of charge. Just drop him off, and we will look after him, you just pay for his drinks.

Sid whose eyesight was suspect at best and whose every shot was followed by cries of "Where did it go?" or "Anyone see where that finished?" asked what all the fuss was about, it's just a pub.

Yes, it is just a pub, a pub called "The Mulchay's Boys" and three of the five cars in the parking lot are police cars!

# CHAPTER 10

# ASSISTANT PROS, VANISHING CLUBS AND THE VENDETTA BEGINS

U nlike most private clubs, we still do a decent business in hard goods. In fact, I have trouble keeping some in the shop. Ping putters in particular just seem to fly out the door; the only problem is no one is actually paying for them. So after staying late one Sunday evening, I set up a tiny camera in the corner of the pro shop. This should be interesting?

It's also mind-numbingly boring. So boring that I quickly hire someone in Islamabad to watch the timecoded video for me and send me back the exact timecode of people leaving or entering the shop with putters. Three dollars an hour well spent!

I don't have to wait long, two days later the first lead is waiting for me in my inbox. Now the hours of my life I thought were wasted on CSI, and numerous other detective shows going back as far as Kojack, Columbo, Ironside and Hill Street Blues finally pay off. My man in Islamabad, Abdul, which not his real name, that's totally unpronounceable, spots a few trends. Namely that clubs seem to disappear on the day a certain teenage boy plays at the club. Searching locally on eBay the putters are easily found. For sale by 18GolferDude@yahoo.com.

I purchase one using the name Dr. Richard Cranium and have it shipped to my friend's house, so no one knows it's me. As I suspected, the kid is dumb enough, or bold enough, to put his return address on the putter. Sure enough, just as in the video, it's the President's nephew, Peter. I wait until he shows up at the club few days later and call the cops. There are 13 stolen putters in his locker, 72 total over the last 18 months. They arrest him and let him go two hours later when his father bails him out.

The President shows up in my office an hour after that and is furious, although not on account of his thieving nephew. He is furious at me that "we" he uses the plural did not handle the matter discreetly. I say nothing as he vents, then leaves, vowing it won't be the last I hear of it and that I might as well start polishing my resume because my time here will be short-lived!

The truth is my time here, now fourteen years plus has been longer than I have ever been anywhere. However, there have been clouds on the horizon for the last two years ever since the President's daughter had the stupidity to marry a golf pro. A younger more malleable type the president could mold into his own man thus consolidating his power base further.

## Dumb Ass Assistant Pros

While yours truly, the head professional has been a model of consistency and reliability, not so with my juniors. I am on my third assistant pro in six months. Third time's a charm I hope!

I tell the second one that the reason I fired the last kid was because he had his hand in the till.

"Oh," he says, "That's not good."

"No, it's not." I agreed.

What perhaps he should have asked is how I caught him? But being young and dumb he did not. Still it shocked me three weeks later when the small but clearly visible eye camera in the corner of the shop showed him pocketing a cash green fee.

The next day I asked him how he thought I caught the last guy stealing. He started at me with his face frozen in panic. I pointed at the little eye in the corner.

"Oh," he says feebly "I saw it but thought it must be fake."

"I am sorry," he mumbled, "I was short on my car payment, I'll pay it back."

Then he put his keys on the table and left. To his credit and my surprise he did send back the $40 about a month later.

The third also had missing inventory problems although he never actually stole anything. Instead, he hid it. Bizarre, I know, but that's what he did.

I have been in this business long enough to do a quick scan of the shop and guestimate my inventory with some accuracy. Therefore it came as no surprise when the inventory did not match sales. Specifically, we had not been paid for a set of Pings, a Callaway driver, several putters, a staff bag and a bunch of shirts in various sizes. Nor did they appear to be in inventory. So, I ordered an old school everything out of the shop inventory check on Monday, and I do mean everything.

The set of Pings that should have been returned as they were not the model we ordered were stashed in the back room behind some old wooden scoreboards. Most of the missing shirts were stuffed in the drawers of a disused desk. The Callaway driver was found in the bathroom broom closet along with a couple of new putters.

Eventually, as if on a scavenger hunt, we found all the missing items.

I confronted the shop girl, but could instantly see that she was as astonished and perplexed as I was.

I confronted assistant number three. He was as guilty and embarrassed as original sin.

"Were you going to sell them?" I asked.

I could see at once he was horrified by the accusation.

"No, of course not!" he stammered.

"Then what?" I asked.

"They were all returns, I tried to do it a couple of times on the computer but I have dyslexia, and I just couldn't get my head around it. I was afraid to screw it up and afraid you'd fire me if you found out, so I just didn't send them back."

"You didn't send them back, and you hid them?" I added.

"Yes," he said quietly

Sometimes real life is stranger than fiction. I left the room, had a cup of coffee, thought hard about it for a few minutes then fired him anyway. I needed someone I could trust. On to assistant number four.

# CHAPTER 11

## BOARD MEETING

I have no idea why they insist I show up at the board meetings. They always ask for my opinion, and they always ignore it. This month for the eighth or ninth time we will be addressing the first three scintillating topics:

- Relaxing the dress code to include, heaven forbid, allowing jeans in the clubhouse!

- Relaxing the cell phone rules to allow them on the course (on non-competition days) and in certain parts of the clubhouse.

- The abolition of the men's only bar which, despite some pussy-whipped wimps, will never pass since the board is made up of twelve men.

- Of more interest, we will also be discussing selling off part of the 14th hole and redesigning it as a drivable par four in a lucrative deal to boost the club's coffers. And provide an even more lucrative access to a proposed new subdivision, run of course, by a close friend of Mr. Formby's.

- Finally, I managed to find an inside champion for changing all the negative wording of our signage to a more user-friendly language. This one was easy it just took a little digging. Mr. Olsen's son has a sign business although we won't be mentioning that little nugget to the rest of the board.

Everyone shows up early for cocktails since the board meeting bar bill is picked up by the club. This leaves a couple of the older double gin drinking members struggling to stay awake before we even start, which we do promptly at 7 pm.

The board is split 50/50 on the jeans issue in a heated debate, with the old guard insisting "standards must be maintained." The new, well in our case, "new" would be a misnomer... let's just say then ones not yet waiting for god, arguing that the world has moved on and that it actually hurts revenue and causes continued embarrassment for members and guests alike.

As usual, they ask for my opinion. I explain that the general trends in the golf industry are towards a more casual environment. Relaxed dress codes, relaxed rules, more emphasis on fun. I say, "I recently had the pleasure of playing Gator Creek, near Sarasota, in Florida. It's a high-end men's club designed for fun! When I arrived, my host was quick to point out the club rules so I would not fall afoul to any and potentially embarrassed him or myself. There were only two rules, printed on a single sheet of paper."

## Club Rules

**1.  Allow faster players to play through**

**2.  Don't piss off the balcony**

There are a few chuckles, a few scowls but when the vote is taken, I vote for jeans, but my vote doesn't count, so it's another hung jury on the jeans matter.

The cell phone changes passed but only because the life of one of the board had just been recently saved by a cell phone when he had suffered a stroke in the middle of the course. His vote broke a four-year deadlock on the matter.

The abolition of the men's only bar failed quickly as usual, but that will not stop the next lady captain adding it to the agenda for the tenth year in a row.

For the re-design of the 14th, the President has pulled out all the stops. We had a presentation from a golf course architect who tells us how much more a fun, short, drivable, risk/reward par four will be for the members. He shows us slides of the 10th at the Belfry, the 8th at Pine Valley, the 12th at TPC and other memorable short holes. Apparently oblivious to that fact that a drivable par four for most of our members would be 220, not 320 and only down-wind!

Next comes the club comptroller who tells us what another $500,000 would do for the club, providing a buffer against future downturns in the economy, which in his opinion is just around the corner.

The President then points out that while this new subdivision will be invisible to the course, it will provide a healthy dose of new blood in the form of future members. "None of us getting any younger," he chuckles, "We must look to sustain the future of our club."

The motion passes, although not without some lingering doubts as to the selling price and Mr. Formby's deeper involvement in the subdivision. This, he artfully deflected, by suggesting that "all of us" might benefit by investing in a lot or two before they were offered to the general public. A hard-fought assurance he has gained from the developer.

Mr. Olsen has put together a short slideshow on the sign issue (Mr. Olsen wouldn't know how to turn a computer on so I did it for him). By pre-arrangement, I offer to advance the slides while he speaks.

The basic thrust of our argument is that all of our on-course and in-clubhouse signs start with the word NO and in some cases are followed by the draconian penalties for not adhering to the said sign.

**For example:**

**No carts signs all over the course** (there are so many I think they are secretly breeding).

**No cart parking** (around the putting green, clubhouse and the range. In fact, all the places a member would want to actually park).

**No chipping**

**No carts in the parking lot**

**No access to the 1st tee via the back of the 18th green**

**No starting on the 10th tee without prior permission from the shop**

**No changing in the parking lot**

**No mulligans**

**No guests before 10 am**

**No Drivers on the range when hitting from the lower tee. Any members caught doing so will face suspension.**

This even though the back fence is 246 yards from the lower tee, which means 90% of the members will have 66 yards to spare!

Mr. Olsen suggests a friendly approach, "Are we not a friendly club?" he asks. That would be very debatable, but of course, there is a chorus of "Hear, hear" in agreement. "Then, rather than barrage our members and guests with negativity should we not request compliance in more friendly tones."

I have seeded the slideshow with a couple of humorous examples to warm them up a bit.

It does. We win ☺

All you have to do to get something passed here, like most clubs, is simply figure out who on the board benefits from the action.

Just like congress really, democracy in action!

# CHAPTER 12

# THE GOOD MEMBER

You may think from reading my true-life account so far that my life is filled only with demanding, rude, ungrateful, prima donnas and pricks, but that's not the case. We do have one good member! Actually, there are a bunch of great members here; it's just they tend to be a lot less vocal and less frequent in their commendations than those who like to bitch on days that end in Y.

Darrin Willard, is the most perfect member a club ever had. A tall, handsome architect who pays his dues on time, brings guests, buys all his equipment through the shop, takes lessons and goes on at least one golf trip a year with me. Oh, and he makes frequent complimentary comments on our Facebook page. He knows the daily BS I have to deal with, or at least some of it, and he frequently gives me the heads up on the locker room scuttlebutt so the worst of it can be headed off at the pass.

"Here I bought this shirt for you in Wales," he says and hands me a white golf shirt with a blue crest on the arm.

I learned a new word over there from one of the caddies he says, do you know what "Sod them," means in the English vernacular?"

"No idea," I admit.

"It's kind of like saying "fuck them!" but is softer and ok to use in polite company.

"Oh," I say, "I'll keep that in mind," and immediately forget since I was pre-occupied with this year's demo day.

## Demo Day

It's a stellar turnout with all the top brands and a large portion of the membership on site. We have brand new Pro V range balls for the event courtesy of Titleist so that everyone gets the very most from the clubs they hit, and therefore stand a better chance of buying them.

There will be none of the balls left in the range barrel by this time next month, and the members will blame their sudden disappearance on guests. Like they blame every unrepaired pitch mark, unfilled divot or unraked trap even on days where there are no guests on the course.

I walk down the line of open tents and kibitz with each of the reps shaking hands, exchanging war stories and offering my help.

The Callaway rep has apparently been instructed to say "Epic" after every drive with his company's product. Which seems like quite a clever idea until someone starts topping it.

We have PXG here for the first time ever. They are conveniently set up next to another of our sponsors Wachovia Bank, so if anyone wants to actually buy a set they can get pre-approved for a loan.

TaylorMade have life-size cutouts of their Tour players with the head missing (particularly apt in Dustin Johnson's case), so the members can get their picture taken as Tour Stars.

Ping has a beat the robot contest, Wilson a trip to Ireland contest and Cleveland a closest wedge challenge. I enter them all just for a bit of fun, knowing if I win I will immediately donate the prize to the juniors fund, before I am hung, drawn and quartered.

Mr. Gross accosts me at the end of the range and asks what's the best deal he can get on the set of irons he just tried. I quote him a price, and he tells me at once he can get them $42 cheaper online!

"Just looked it up," he says triumphantly waiving his cell phone as proof!"

"How did you hit that set online?" I ask trying to hide my frustration.

"What," he says puzzled, "I didn't obviously!"

"Is it worth the risk? I ask, "To buy a set you haven't hit when we obviously we have a set right here on the range that you love?"

"They are all the same, aren't they?" he asked.

"Well, that's what the manufactures would like you to believe for sure. But some just don't get sprinkled with the same pixie dust." I say barely managing to keep it jovial.

"Pixie dust!" he exclaims. "Can you match that price?"

"I can custom fit them for you and only charge you half price for the fitting, how's that?" I offer.

"Not as good as a $42 discount," he says.

"Ok," I say resigned, "I'll match the online price."

And stick it to you some other way you cheap bastard, I think as I capitulate and hate myself for doing it. What he doesn't realize is that lousy $42 is going to cost him big time. No sliding on a late afternoon cart free for "just a couple of holes." No sliding on a second round guest fee. No tee times exactly when he wants them, yep that $42 bucks he thinks he saved are gonna cost him plenty!

Fortunately, Darrin Willard shows up and snaps me out of my negativity. He hits every club on the range and buys an entirely new set of irons and woods at list no questions asked. His third new set in two years. "Epic."

All in all, another good demo day!

## The Best Course in Wales

A week later I am in the shop re-arranging the shirts.

"Is that in Greece?" asked one of the members?

"What?" I asked in genuine surprise having no context to go on.

He pointed at my white golf shirt sleeve where the words Llamehtdos CC we embroidered in large green letters.

"Oh that," I said, "No, it's a club I once played in Wales."

"Wales?"

"Yes," I said, "While not as well-known as Scotland or Ireland there are some great links golf in Wales, St David's, Aberdovey, Porthcawl, Nyfin and all at half the price or less of their more famous counterparts!"

"And this Llamehtdos CC, is that one of the best?"

"No, not really," I said, "It's just a place one of our members had a lot of fun at," I said with a smile.

"Maybe you should organize a trip there, the rest of the Sparrow group is looking for a summer trip!"

"I don't think they have summer in Wales, Doc."

"What?" he said then cracked as rueful smiled as he caught on I was pulling his leg

"Do you fly into London?" he asked

"You could but Manchester in much closer about two hours to the best courses in North Wales," I replied.

"Would you mind sending me a quick email with a recommended Itinerary? He asked.

"Sure Doc, how long do you want to go for ten days including two travel days?" I asked, like a seasoned travel pro!

"Yes, excellent! You are good man Jerry. I hope all the members appreciate you as much as I do!"

I smile, THEY DON'T!

Now I can add travel agent to the long list of additional jobs I do. By the time I add website links to each course another 15-20 minutes of my life will have evaporated on that "quick" email.

There are two guests in the shop from England; one has an earring in his left ear the other is covered in more tattoos than a Maori warrior or even David Beckham. They are standing just a few feet away from me sniggering, and earring man is pointing at the full-length mirror in the corner of the pro shop where I am standing. In it is my reflection as I show Mrs. Marconi a new Jamie Sadock shirt that would look amazingly good on her 20-year old granddaughter and about as out of place on her as the Bible in a hookers hands!

"Llamehtdos CC," says one English guy to the other, "Do you get it?"

"No," says the other.

"Look," he points at the mirror where the lettering is reversed.

"SOD-THEM-ALL-CC," he says howling.

I quickly turn my back to the mirror as Darren's little joke has been exposed, not that Mrs. Marconi has the faintest idea what's going on but "sod them all" when spelled backward comes out sounding like a perfect Welsh town, which of course you won't find on any map. It's like those Disney artists who can't help throwing in the occasional sex innuendo into the scenes of their hit movies. It was just Darren Willard's little way of helping me get through the day with a smile on my face.

Outside, the English guy with the earing jumps on a golf cart and floors it sending it straight backward into the coke machine and almost crushing the cart boy in the process. The machine is a totaled; the cart will live to fight another day. The guest is so shaken up he decides to walk. I really must talk to the cart boys again about leaving the carts in neutral.

# CHAPTER 13

## SLOWLY GROWING
## THE GAME

This year I've been involved in several of the initiatives to grow the game pushed by the various governing bodies especially those aimed at minorities and women.

First, we partnered with the First Tee and invited 40 ghetto kids to use our range for a few weeks over the summer, two nights a week. We provided free instruction, free range balls and free clubs that were kindly donated by our members. We also provided free bottles of booze, towels, cologne, shirts, shoes, blazers, two golf carts, a mower and just about anything else that wasn't nailed down. Nor was it officially donated by anyone. The kids had a blast, the clubhouse manager a stroke and our insurance agent threatened to cancel our policy if we ever did it again.

The 22 ladies we invited as part of our initiative to get women on the course was more successful. We got one new member. A DUI followed by a lawsuit for serving another three glasses of wine when according to her "we should have cut her off" and a sexual harassment lawsuit aimed at the assistant lady pro who apparently made a pass at one of the ladies, who knew? At least Joe Speakman is happy. He's one of our members, a lawyer and got both cases.

For a while, I toyed with the idea of a special program to attract Native American's, Eskimo's and Hawaiian's to the game as I am sure I could have found some support for such a bold plan within the ranks of the USGA or PGA. Instead, next year I have vowed to go back to the shockingly out of favor practice of trying to attract some of the ten million, white, middle-aged men who already have clubs in their garage back to the game. Not sexy, not politically correct, not something that's going to get any press, but maybe just maybe a better use of my time and effort? I mean they have clubs, they have balls, they have golf shoes, they have played before it can't be that hard to get some of them back to the course?

## Flag at Half Mast

The flag is at half-mast again this week for the third time, and it's only Wednesday. Last year the flag flew at half-mast a record 57 times. Lots of clubs these days are dying we just seem to be better at than most. Which I guess is why some drunk joker on April 1 replaced the flag at a permanent state of half-mast by chopping it in half. And while I admit I did permit myself a small smile when I first noticed it, the membership aging as it was went nuclear.

The police were called, the security company was called, all the security guards on duty were called, I was called, the assistants were called and a full-scale inquiry was launched with the president promising to get to the bottom of it if it was the last thing he did. Which the way things are going it just may well be.

## Desperately Seeking Members

We desperately need new members so much, I bought a book on the subject aptly titled *Desperately Seeking*

*Members.* In its pages were some clever ideas like having a marketing budget, using social media to tap into the friends of members and training someone to actually sell memberships. We, of course, do none of these radical things we are strictly a build it, and they will come operation!

Still, despite the fact that we need new blood, it seems we don't need just anybody…

It had to happen eventually. Someone proposed an Ex-NFL player for membership. He was a wide receiver with the Dolphins, Jets and Raiders and a possible future hall of famer. I played with him once in a celebrity event, and he seemed like a pretty nice guy, not the prima donna or gangster type that so many athletes turn out to be. Funny too, as he banged a seven iron 15 yards over the first green from 170, he looked at me shrugged apologetically and said, "A Rodney King."

"A Rodney King?" I asked.

"Yeah you know brother," he says laughing, "Over clubbed!"

Apparently, his father had taken half his money from his initial multi-million dollar contract and invested it with a legitimate broker. Which meant he still had half his money left. Now he just played golf and did the occasional TV appearance just to keep his name out there.

There was only one problem, the club currently has no black members and no one it seemed in these days of enlightenment wanted to be the first to say YES. Sad but true!

I had suggested we offer honorary memberships to Halle Berry, Rhianna, and Beyoncé to take the curse off it a bit. But the joke was lost on the board as none of them had ever heard of them. I even thought about throwing in Michelle Obama, but that would have gone down like a lead balloon and called into question my patriotism with everyone in the club except Hal Weinstein.

They did not want to say yes, but at the same time, they knew the adverse publicity the club would get if they turned him down would be devastating. This called for a special closed-door meeting of the membership committee.

In the end, they come up with a compromise by offering him an honorary membership on account of all his local charity work. This means that he does not have to go through the normal channels and face probable rejection. By our rules, that makes him a full member but ineligible to vote or invite new members. He likes the fact they give him a free membership and couldn't care less. Sort of a backhanded win, win. Progress? Hardly!

# CHAPTER 14

## AUGUSTA AT LAST

For some players, collecting golf clubs, memorabilia or even memberships is not what makes them tick. Their raison d'etre is getting to play the world's greatest courses. Ticking off the Top 100 is what gives them a buzz.

Each year, various publications produce their list of the Top 100 courses with multiple sub-lists by country, state and course type. Many golfers make playing all these courses their life's mission and what a mission it is.

Since the list is ever changing, many pick a certain year and go with that list as their goal. Others strive only to play all the courses that, for example, have hosted the British Open, which is eminently do-able since there are only nine on the present roster and access to all is possible. Thus making that goal a good short-term mission. In fact, playing the top 100 in the UK is a far easier task than the US, since although most clubs are private, all but a tiny few allow outside play.

In the USA playing the Top 100 is indeed a worthy life-long mission and while the first few fall easily in your home state or at places like Pebble where the only barrier is steep green fees, the mission gets increasingly difficult as you start to target the hallowed grounds of Pine Valley, Cypress Point, and Augusta. Still, if it were easy, it would take all the fun out of it!

Real aficionados and collectors look for charity tournaments, outings, and special one-time raffles for charitable purposes to find entry to some clubs. LinkedIn must be worked, corporate suppliers must be chosen carefully, and events must be entered to expand your network of potential sponsors. One must also be prepared to host others first and being a member of a high-quality course will, of course, be a big help. Because I was, I was able to cross off the number one course early in my quest.

**It doesn't get any better than this!**

I don't know if you remember the old beer commercials were a group of young guys after a long day hiking in the mountains are sitting down enjoying the amazing vistas and a cold beer. One guy remarks "It just doesn't get any better than this." Suddenly the Swedish bikini team parachute in. Well, that happened to me!

It all started when a guy I once played golf with called me late one night to ask if I could get him and six of his friends a game at my club as they were in town on business. I set it up with a couple of my friends, and a few weeks later we had a great day of golf playing both courses. One of the group just happened to be a member of the legendary Augusta National Club, consistently ranked as the number one or two course in the world depending on who's list you follow. He left with an invitation to play there the following fall, probably not realizing that I had fantasized about playing there since lying in bed with the flu at thirteen and my father brought home the World Atlas of Golf.

Eventually, I pulled through the gates and started to get that tingly feeling. You know what I mean, the one that the players talk about when driving down Magnolia

Lane. Or the one that anyone can experience walking over the bridge at the 18th hole of St. Andrews. I was dropped off at my room and whisked off to what must surely be one of the world's best practice areas set deep in the woods complete with Titleist practice balls. After 45 minutes of beating balls, I returned just in time to meet my host and his friends, whereupon we changed for dinner.

Dinner was no less spectacular than the course with some of the finest lamb I have ever tasted accompanied by an excellent Cabernet.

The day started early as players began to hit the showers at 6:30. By seven it was off to the range followed by a quick breakfast and introduction to our caddies all of whom are characters in their own right. Mine was an ex-professional soccer player, ex-golf pro, had a Ph.D. and was traveling the country writing a book on "The American Caddie."

At 7:50 am exactly I stood ready to hit my tee shot down the first hole a daunting task. While the fairways are very generous, missing them makes the hole increasingly difficult. In fact, in five rounds I never made even a single par from a drive that did not find the short grass. You think you'd make one by accident, but such is the penalty for poor play on this McKenzie layout. A little less than four hours later I had accomplished my personal goal, I had broken 80 with an almost solid 77 from the member tees, with only three three-putts!

Sunday was another scorcher, but we decided to play all the way from the tips. I bogeyed 18 for a 79, meeting another goal of breaking 80 all five rounds. After a shower, everyone started on their way out of town. Since my original flight was at 7 pm and it was only 1 pm, I had time to kill, so I got on my cell phone and started to try and make better flight arrangements. None were available (are they ever?), but I decided to head down for a long wait at the airport. Within minutes the caddie master had summoned the club's van, and I was on my way. In the air-conditioned comfort of the bus, I got one last look at the course as we drove to the guest cottages to pick up three other passengers.

After a short wait, two guests and a member entered the bus. We exchanged the usual pleasantries and talked about how great the course was. One last look at the 18th as we drove out of the gates was captured on my new digital camera for posterity. What a great weekend!

Then just when you thought it couldn't get any better, it did! No, the Swedish bikini team did not miraculously appear on the bus, that stuff only happens on TV, this was better!

One of the three men on the bus had overheard me making my last ditched effort on my cell phone to get a flight that didn't get me in at midnight.

"Where are you heading?" he asked.

"Newark," I answered.

"Just come with us then," he said

"I am sorry," I said, unsure by what he meant.

"We have a Learjet, and there is plenty of room. We are going to drop my son off in Newark and then fly up to Vermont."

"Ok, thanks," I said nonchalantly with a warm smile.

Like people I have never met in my life often offer me a thousand-mile ride in their private jets.

Checking bags took five minutes and getting airborne took at least another five. All the seats were window seats, and there were bottles of Sam Adams on ice in a cooler. I got to Newark a four full hours before my plane was even scheduled to depart Atlanta. They had even called ahead to book a town car for me to take me home.

You can't make this shit up! Some days the universe just aligns even for a lowly golf pro like me!

# CHAPTER 15

## THEY WOULDN'T REALLY HIRE A BIG SUIT MANAGEMENT COMPANY WOULD THEY?

T he club is losing money and considering hiring one of the big suit management companies. Like spending ten grand a month on adding their logo to everything will solve anything?

The upside of this news is a massive increase in cooperation between myself, the club manager, head chef and Scottish twat of greenkeeper. All of whom know that should we allow this to come to pass, none of us will make it through the first day. It's a well-known management company tactic to fire the pro and promote the assistant. This happens in name only, not salary, and they continue this trend through each position at the club saving more than enough to pay their inflated fees.

Each of us is tasked with finding dirt on the top three candidates in our respective areas of expertise and passing the info along to a friendly face on the board. This proves to be ridiculously easy with fifteen minutes on Google.

Broken promises, missed goals, member lawsuits, numerous unfair dismissals and a couple of fraud cases just for starters.

John Parkinson is our main inside guy and as a trial lawyer, the perfect person to face down Big Suit Number 1. He has just given a flawless presentation of bullshit, complete with stunning slides, video, and music. This guy could have a future as an Oscar host, tall, square-jawed sporting an Armani suit, slicked-back gray hair and steel-rimmed glasses like some character from Dallas or Dynasty.

John stands up to ask his question, and it's a doozy from the chef and greenskeeper design to hit him right in the gut. "Do you have a preferred vendor program that provides your management company with fees in return for the management company recommending their products to your clients?"

Big Suit's face flushes red; he looks nervous. Obviously, he has never had to answer a question this direct before, since he obviously doesn't have the answer. Finally, he stutters, "We do have a preferred vendor program, but I am not sure of the details on how each vendor is selected? I do know they are best in their class."

John presses on as if Big Suit is an Enron accountant in the witness box. "When you say best in their class do you mean they are universally recognized as the best vendor like say Legendary Marketing is for golf marketing or do you mean they are the ones who pay you the most money to be a preferred vendor?"

"We only deal with the top companies!" he says hoping that non-answer would kill the question. It did not.

"Sorry, I just want to be clear on this point. Are saying that you don't take kickbacks, commissions or fees from 3rd party vendors?"

"No, I did not say that," he squeals on the verge of totally losing his composure. "I think there are some companies that provide us with rebates."

"I see," says John rubbing a hand across his face as he pretends to mull this over, "That's not a very objective way to select the best vendors, is it?"

"They are all quality vendors," he insists lamely.

"Quite," says John, "But would it not be more fair to pass these fees along to your clients' since you are already getting paid ten grand a month for management, which presumably would include getting the best deals you can from vendors for your clients? Seems like a direct conflict of interest to me!"

Big Suit is squirming like a ten year who needs to pee badly. "I can find out the details and get back to you! Do you have any other questions?" he quickly adds no doubt hoping the answer is "No."

"I do, will there be any other costs to the club other than your rather large fees?"

"Well, we will have to upgrade your club's technology." Says Suit #1.

"You mean get the latest versions of all the software we have?" Asks John.

"No, no we completely replace everything from scratch, so it matches all our other clubs and makes life easier for all of us."

"For-all-of-us," John repeats slowly with emphasis and continues, "Speaking of software, it was brought to my attention that your company's website is quite dated and you don't have much of a Facebook presence. Can you explain that?

"Yes, we like to see how things develop before going full on we think the verdict is still out on the internet 2.0 and are waiting for 3.0 before we make a definitive next move. As for social media, the consensus at head office is that it will never really catch on with golfers. I mean none of our executive VP's are active on Facebook or Twitter, and we are all pretty switched on guys, so I think that tells you something about what the golf market thinks of social media."

"Well according to my son who works in the internet field and looked at your stuff, you guys are somewhere back in Bedrock when it comes to online marketing," states John flatly, "Which won't help us much in getting new members."

Flustered again, like Jack Nicholson in a *Few Good Men,* Big Suit #1 blurts out before he can stop himself, "It's worth remembering. No one will ever second guess your decision to hire us because we are so BIG. We may be behind the times on many things going on in the industry today, but we are a safe bet. By the time your club fires us, it will be some other boards problem, not yours!" He quickly folds up his laptop and leaves.

Big Suit #2 is not as slick, but he's more affable in his approach.

"Since you are so sure of your ability to help us perhaps you'd be willing to do it on a pay for performance basis?" asks John.

"I am sure we can help you, but that's not how we operate." Says Big Suit #2.

"Can you show me the marketing strategy you have developed for another similar course?"

"No, that would be proprietary."

"Ok, what's the first thing you will do?"

"Branding."

"When you say branding do you mean branding the club or your management company?"

"Sorry?" Suit #2 says quizzically.

"Well it's just my friend is a member at a private club that used to be managed by your group and when you guys took over the most obvious change was you reprinted everything at a cost of over $50,000, so you could add your logo to all the collateral. Even had three logo stickers per golf cart with your name and just one of the club's crest. A new member would have had difficulty finding the name of the club."

He smiles "I think you are exaggerating a little," he says.

"Oh no," says John with a smile and pulls out his cell phone with a picture of the clubs cart fleet adorned in more logos than a NASCAR, all with the management company's name. Provided by the ousted pro at the other club along with some other juicy tidbits.

"When people know a club is being managed by a company like us it attracts members." Protests Suit #2.

"Really, I never joined a club in my life because it was being managed by a certain management company?" Said John in an astonished tone.

"People do," he insisted weakly and then packs up and leaves slightly crestfallen but unlike Big Suit #1, still wearing a forced smile.

Suit #3 is not in a suit at all. In fact, he's got a dark blue polo shirt and a sports coat. He starts by telling us he used to be a golf pro but realizing potential there was waning got into management (funny his real name was "Peter"). This he tells us gives him unique insight into running a club.

He'll at least know how to fold shirts and sell mars bars I thought, but John jumps in before I can say anything.

"How quickly can you turn our club around?"

"Rome wasn't built in a day, the economy is tough, and you are in a very competitive market. These things take time to do properly so we will need a five-year contract with an option for another ten years."

The prospect of a 15 year thankfully kills his chances without any further questions. Most of his company's portfolio was low-end money losing muni's anyway!

The board decides to kick the question down the line and see how we do next year. The suits are all out ten grand for flying in and doing their dog and pony show, and we all keep our jobs for at least another 12 months. Mission accomplished, now after a celebratory pint together as four musketeers, we can all go back to business, as usual, undermining each other's efforts in peace!

# CHAPTER 16

## EVERY DOCTOR'S SECRET FANTASY

D r. Travis wants to buy a golf course in Florida as an investment, to go along with his llama farm, his salmon fishery and the only Italian restaurant in New Jersey serving Ostrich pizza. A great heart surgeon he is said to be, a great investor he is not, which is why he wants to take me down there on a rented jet to look the place over and tell him what I think.

He, of course, won't give two hoots to what I think but I fancy a trip to Florida this time of year to warm the bones, and I'll stay over next week for the PGA show in Orlando. We land the Citation at a small commercial airstrip near Ocala and drive into the countryside for 30 minutes. It's nice, not like Florida at all, rolling hills, mature oaks and hardly a palm tree in sight!

The downside of this idyllic scene is apart from the odd subdivision between the rolling fields of the horse farms there aren't really that many people. In fact, there are more horses than people and last time I checked horses don't play golf... although the way things are going, maybe golf polo will be next!

We pull into the parking lot, and every pore screams 1970. Small, flat-roofed clubhouse, a parking lot that had its first holes in the Ford administration and golf carts that were young when Arnie was still winning golf tournaments.

The place was beat up, milked dry for every dime that could be had without investing a single cent in anything. I bet you a Benji they have an old Fore reservations POS and a GolfNow website that says Welcome to Our Club, with sales copy so weak it couldn't sell John Daley a beer.

I check behind the counter; it does, nailed that one! Add to their shitty marketing and management system an irrigation system with more holes in it than the Swiss cheese they put on their $4 burgers and what you have here is a genuine money eating pit, cleverly disguised as a golf course!

Of course, none of this deters the good doctor one iota, he sees possibilities everywhere. The mildew smelling wreck of a clubhouse could be turned into a Jamaican themed Reggae hut with jerk chicken and Bob Marley in the background. Lots of color, paint the chairs, tables, and walls. Pink, red, green gold. He thinks he can give the place a new life through an intravenous injection of Sherwin Williams paint!

He excitedly heads outside to an ancient cart whose seat is 50% duct tape, and we head out to the first tee.

"It's a good layout."

It's such a cliché, but it really is decent looking track. A nice blend of doglegs left and right, a few ponds, a good size lake and mature oak trees dripping with the Spanish moss that looks so good at dawn but will eventually strangle them to death.

I'd say based on the greenkeepers budget the guy deserves a medal. The course is in decent shape for an operation that obviously needs a loan to buy a box of golf balls.

We finish touring all 18 with the Doc snapping pictures on his iPhone like a Japanese tourist.

"What do you think?" he says excitedly as we find a seat the in the shade of the empty patio, the smell of stale cigarettes in the air.

"Doc, I love you, but you are nuts. This place isn't worth $500,000. There is at least a million dollars in deferred maintenance and even when you fix it up who's going to play here Trigger, Mr. Ed, Champion the Wonder Horse and their friend Black Beauty?"

"They were all a bit before your time," he says with a hint of surprise. "They are asking 1.5 million but I think I could steal it for $900,000."

"Doc, you would not be stealing it at $300,000 unless you can develop it which you already said you can't!"

"The area is growing," he protested.

"The area is growing grass!" I say.

"The pro says they don't do any marketing."

"Of course they don't none of these clubs do they think GolfNow will make it rain gofers! Instead, it just helps them give away tee times for less than $10 bucks, although looking at this place that might be a shade too high."

A large, middle-aged guy, with a big gut, wearing all black and Ray-Ban's that made him look like an extra in a mafia movie comes outside and introduces himself with a big smile.

"I'm Joe," he says, then quickly adds his punchline "But not your average Joe! I've been the pro here for the last 12 years since Mr. Darcy bought it. You guys have any questions I could help you with?"

"How many rounds do you do?' I ask.

"About 30,000," then adds, "But a lot of the member rounds aren't really tracked they just drive their carts out and play."

"How many members?" I query.

"At the peak, we had almost 400, now it's down to 125. Sorry 124, Fred Pickering died Monday," he says as he shakes his head.

"Revenue?"

"$925,000…and shrinking," he says. "Used to do almost double that."

Back when the world was young, I thought.

"Profit?"

He takes off his shades and looks at me like I'm the dumbest schmuck in Christendom.

"There hasn't been a year this place made money since the crash of 2008, year after he bought it. Loses $150-200k a year, every year!"

"Can it make money?" I ask, expecting the answer to be no.

He looks uncertain, "Well, we don't do any marketing obviously, that would help. There is a rumor the city is going to shut down their course, and our main competitor is on life support."

"What and you are not?" I ask with a laugh.

He grins, "Mr. Darcy is a wealthy man."

"Then he's probably not dumb enough to keep pumping two hundred thousand a year into this…" I was about to say dump but catch myself and say, "Place!"

"This is good news," says Doc who apparently heard nothing except the two nearby courses might be closing. We leave in our rented Cadillac and go look at the other two courses. Both of the same vintage and both in the same shape, maybe even a little bit worse.

Doc insists we fly to Tampa to have lunch at his favorite seafood place adding $1,000 in jet fuel and an extra 90 minutes of jet rental to our lunch tab before he returns north. Must be nice!

At lunch, he asks me if I am willing to be his Pro/Manager if he buys it. I say I might take the job for twice what I am being paid now, a house on the course and my own horse (the horse was a joke), but only if I could not talk him out of buying it first!

"Splendid!" he says.

I can only roll my eyes. If I took the job I'd make good money on my terms, for two or three years until he ditched it and then be a 50-year-old golf pro looking for one more gig in Florida. Me and the rest of the East Coast, Mid-West and Deep South. Plus, it's the lowest paying state in the union for golf pros.

Doc flies home, and I grab a rental car to head over to the PGA show in Orlando. They have a special on Mustang convertibles, so I grab a cherry red one, sure to impress any kid over 50!

# CHAPTER 17

# KID IN A CANDY STORE - PGA SHOW BOUND

I t's that time of year again when the world of golf descends on Orlando, Florida for the annual PGA show at the Orange County Convention Center. Hotel prices triple, I-drive becomes a parking lot, restaurants have a two-hour wait, and you can be sure it's the worst weather week of the year, hurricanes excepted. You just don't expect it to be cold in Florida but the third week of January always is.

The show is big, but not nearly as big as it was a decade ago, back then it was maybe three times the size. It was so big you could not even speed walk the whole show in a day. That was back in the dot-com days when they had 44 companies selling tee sheets alone. The Ashworth party was the hot ticket where they blew a half million on drinks and a rock band. At 5 pm you'd head from the show across the road to the Peabody Bar (now the Hyatt) where it took at least 45 minutes to get a drink, but you would meet everyone in the golf industry in an evening. Jack, Tiger, Greg, Gary, Fazio, Ledbetter, Trump, Dye, Crenshaw, Faldo, McCord, trick shot legend, Dennis Walters and his dog plus the Troon, Kemper and Casper boys. They all passed through there on at least one of the evenings.

It's not as good now as they opened a far larger bar on the other side of the hotel and the party is split between two places. The Peabody ducks have taken their last walk, and attendance is half what it used to be. Still, it's somewhere you have to go if you are a golf pro because everybody who is anyone will be there, if not every year at least every third year.

Although it's a trade show and not open to the public the aisles are jammed with club members wearing "buyer" badges scooping up the freebies and anything that isn't nailed down into plastic bags branded with this year's sponsor. Our "buyers" badge went to Hal Formby, who I am trying to avoid like the plague.

Unlike many of my peers, I try to walk every aisle and actually look at what's there rather than keep to the middle of the aisle with my head down so I don't actually make contact with any of the vendors who might want to tell me about their product.

Who I really feel sorry for are the poor bastards with the golf inventions or the training aids. The next "big thing," all of whom shot their entire wad on a $15,000 trip to Orlando. All expecting to sell thousands of units or get bought out by one of the big guys who will surely recognize the genius of their contraption. Instead, they go home with a handful of sales worth $497 and should count themselves lucky.

I pride myself on being a bit of a clothes guy. Not GQ like Rod Cook, or pristine like Larry Strazel but fashionable a little outside the box, trendy, cutting-edge. Which means I am always disappointed by the massive merchandise area. Under Armour, Nike, Adidas, take your pick everyone has the same solids with a different logo. Everyone the same stripes with a different logo. Where the hell is the innovation?

Back in 80's you had the iconic Borg, striped Fila shirts with the little metal stud buttons. In the 90's the Greg Norman shirts with the huge multi-colored shark design and metal buttons to show off your manliness. There was the very stylish Le Coq Sportif stuff worn by Nick Price before he had a shirt brand of his own, which although high quality, looked just like everyone else's. So lost was I in reminiscing about the perfect shirt that I turned onto the next aisle and walked right into him, Hal Formby, El Presidente. He insists we meet for dinner. I make every excuse in the book but eventually settle on Friday night.

I hustle off to hear the opening PGA show address from a basketball coach who never ran a club in his life. Last year it was a football coach, the year before a motivational speaker who obviously didn't even play golf. So bad were his puns and misuse of golfing terminology, I wonder why they don't just hire Andrew Wood or Jim Keegan or someone who actually knows something about the golf business?

I follow up the keynote address by attending an educational session from a pro who really does know how to run an awesome operation. Unfortunately, he does not know how to speak in public and is so nervous in front of the 80 or so people in the room he can hardly function the button to move his slides. As he drones on in a monotone voice, he is peppered by frequent shouts from the audience to "Speak up, "We can't hear you" and "Could you repeat that!"

I try one more, and that's me done with "education" for another show. It's titled **Marketing to Today's Golfer** by a good looking blonde in a pinstripe business skirt, suit thing, whatever you call that. She is polished, professional, passionate and full of shit! All she talks about is logos and brand not one idea, not even by accident, in forty-five minutes on how to put more players on the course!

Who vets these people?

Still, there is nothing like the show for meeting old friends and making new ones. Even after all these years walking the isles and fondling all the new equipment still gives me a thrill like a kid in a candy store. I look at a couple of the apps, try out a massage chair, buy yet another pair of in-sole thingumajigs to soothe my aching feet and spend an hour hitting different irons in the net range. I'm about ready for some new tools. A good full day at the show, now it's time to cross the street and see who I know at the Peabody (Hyatt) bar.

I grab a couple of Stella's, chat with a few groups, cruise the old and new bars then head out to I-drive. I meet El Presidente at the Funky Monkey, a high-end bistro and wine bar a short walk from the convention center. They had a special on wines made by golfers. He holds up the list and reads it out loud.

"Greg Norman Merlot?"

"Do they have any Yellow Tail?" I asked. He ignores me and continues.

"Gary Player, Black Night?"

"A bit quirky" I shoot back.

"Luke Donald, Cab?" he continues.

"Solid, but a bit too middle of the fairway" I suggest.

"Jan Stephenson Reserve? I never knew she did wine." He remarks and continues the commentary without waiting for my response, "I would certainly have liked to have tasted a younger vintage."

Indeed I thought to myself, but didn't she have an alcohol problem? No, maybe that was Laura Baugh. He continued reading the list.

"Ernie Els, Big Easy Blend?" I hear that's a good one he says excitedly, but there are a couple more.

"Good wines, in fact, I've been to his vineyard in Stellenbosch," I respond.

"Frost Par Excellence."

"Now that's a great wine and from someone who doesn't just put his name on the bottle. Did you know he grew up in the wine business - his father owned a vineyard?"

"Really?"

"Indeed, how much is it?"

It's very reasonable, and the club will be picking up my expenses anyway. We ordered a bottle and a few small plates. Trying to force some conversation I asked, "See anything at the show that caught your eye?"

"The booth babes on the Puma stand!" He said excitedly.

I tried again. "Any products?"

"I did have a go in one of those golf simulators and thought that might be a nice addition to the club for the winter months!"

I raised an eyebrow, "That's a very good Idea" I said. So good in fact that I had already suggested it for the last three years.

After a couple of glasses of wine he said casually, "Jerry, I wonder if you have thought about retiring?"

I almost spat out my wine, "How would I do that at 46 on the salary the club pays me?"

"Well," he says " I could arrange for a lump sum, maybe move down to Florida, play a little more golf. I am sure you could easily get a position at any number of places. I mean most of our members have a second homes down there, and I know you are popular with the ladies," he says raising an eyebrow!

"But not with you?" I ask blankly and smile a sardonic grin.

"Jerry," he says with open hands "It's nothing personal you know it's just I would like to be near my daughter and to get her back here. Jason, her husband, needs a job.

"He needs my job?" I ask as casually as possible.

"Look, I know we haven't always seen eye to eye but just think about it. I can ask the board for a year's salary, and ask around to see who's got a  position opening up in the sun! It's time you had a change!"

"I'll tell you what," I say, "Get me director of golf at Doral or Head Pro at Seminole and I'll think about it."

I excuse myself to go to the restroom but head back to the Peabody bar instead. Old habits die hard everyone still calls it the Peabody. I leave him to pick up the check and enjoy the show. He wanted somewhere with girls, and they have a great show burlesque type show at the Monkey, every Friday night. It's quite risqué for a place in Orlando where the shadow of the mouse flanks every decision not deemed "family friendly." The thing is the girls in the show which struts up and down between the tables are the type you might find in the wrong bar in Bangkok. I hope he enjoys it!

# CHAPTER 18

## PORN GATE & PAYBACK

My five-year-old club computer is on the blink again, and they call our part-time IT guy to come and get it working again. I hardly use it for anything except tee times and the POS system since it's so archaic. So it struck me as quite odd when I was told that the board wished to see me on Thursday night to discuss allegations of misuse of club property, specifically the club's computer.

As I have said, I had known for some time that the club President was trying to oust me since I had his nephew arrested for stealing 72 putters and so he could move his golf pro son-in-law into my position, but this took things to new lows.

The IT guy who no doubt was in collusion with the club President had found some pornographic images in my deleted emails while "fixing" my computer and he felt it was only right to report these to the board.

I often wonder why the fuck Tiger did not have a throwaway cell phone. How could he be dumb enough to use his main phone to communicate with all those girls? Likewise, were I the sort of person that spent hours at work surfing porn sites I would have done it on my personal iPad, NOT the club's computer. Did the board really think I was that fucking dumb?

Apparently so.

The 12 of them sit there like judge and jury. The President speaks, "Jerry, I'll get straight to the point, no need to beat around the bush, I want to get to the bottom of this."

"For Christ's sake, get on with it!" I thought.

"We are very concerned about a number of pornographic images found on your computer, which as you know is club property. What do you have to say for yourself?"

"I'd say that I can't control what people send me via email and that it's no big deal. They come in, I delete most without opening them. Others from people I know,

I glance at them since before I open them I can't tell what's inside, and I quickly delete them."

"I would say it's a very big deal," says his highness the President (all Hail Caesar).

"Look, there are only a few, mainly from members. There is someone out there that's signing me up for some porn newsletters in payback from some perceived slight. Probably your nephew." I suggest helpfully.

"Who are these members?" he asks gruffly clearly ruffled that I have brought up his nephew again.

"I really don't think we should go into that; I just delete them." I protest, knowing what a Pandora's box this will be win or lose.

"I insist we should." He says resolutely.

"Fair enough." I say, prepared to fight, "I have printed out one of the deleted emails which shows two naked blondes, obviously, lesbians playing intimately with an Odyssey putter."

"That's exactly what I am talking about" he yells triumphantly, "filth!"

"It was sent to me by the lady captain. You can see her email address clearly in the top left corner, ladycaptian2018@gmail.com."

"What are you saying?" Scoffed the President.

"What I am saying that this particular image was sent to me by the lady captain. In this case no doubt by mistake, apparently, her female partner is also called Jerry, easy mistake to make." I say as I smile and open my hands.

"This next one was sent to me by Jack Raymar, the milk baron who as you know lent the club $500,000 last year. He sends me his "pic of the day" every day despite my repeated requests that he not share. He thinks it's funny."

"This one…"

"Enough" yells the president slightly red-faced and obviously scared at who I will embarrass next. "That will be all; we shall consider the matter closed!"

Of course, that was just the beginning. The lady captain was now a mortal enemy, but someone had to take the fall, and it sure wasn't going to be me.

The only thing I had on my side was it was near the end of her term, and she had just accepted a new job out of state which is why I picked her in the first place. She and Jerri with an "I" would be moving. I never actually showed they board any of Jack's emails and I could square it up with him in person anyway so "Ok" there.

The President, on the other hand, had been outfoxed and embarrassed yet again by his own hand. Why it had not occurred to him to check the source of the emails was beyond my comprehension, couldn't have been much of a lawyer!

## Payback

It's a shame, so many golf clubs get brought down to such petty politics and squabbles, but one of us would have to go, and it would be my turn to take the next shot!

For months I had fantasies about how I could catch him, for he was a notorious cheat on and off the course.

I even thought of hiring a private detective and catching him with one of the waitresses or the cart girl who often visited the condo he owned just outside the gates. Then, a far simpler high tech solution came to my door.

It apparently never occurred to the arrogant bastard that the drone flying back and forth across the course which he complained about bitterly on two occasions was filming him. I had hired the firm to do new 3D graphics for our website with the stipulation that I wanted to catch this old basted cheating in the process. They loved the idea and took to it like Bond on a mission. They filmed him on three separate occasions, kicking his ball out from behind a tree, improving his lie in the rough and dropping balls when he couldn't find his.

Taking the money from his playing partners every time, which of course I checked.

BINGO!

I invited the President into my office and showed him the footage on my laptop. He sat there silently seething. Then he shocked me one more time.

"How much do you want?" he sneered.

The arrogant bastard actually thought I wanted money, imagine!

"I don't want anything I just want you to resign and fade away like the cockroach lawyer you are," I announced as smugly as possible. "Health reasons, plenty of other clubs you can join in the area. Then no one but you and I ever need to know about this little incident. Least of all Frankie Sacarletti whom I have heard you have beat for quite a lot of money lately!" He visibly twitched at the sound of Frank's name. Frank actually owns a chain of hair salons in New Jersey, but he always liked to hint that he might, you know, have some connections if anyone ever needs a favor.

Meanwhile, it was me who finally gave the President an offer he couldn't refuse ☺

Ten of the remaining guys on the board are "Pro-Jerry" so now I can go back to being a middle-aged golf pro in relative peace waiting out my time until the club presents me with a golden putter.

Doc's Florida deal which had been dragging on for months finally fell through when a hurricane removed the clubhouse and half the trees on the course.

The first tee is open; it's 4:30 so you know what I'm going to do? Something I haven't done in weeks. I'm going to tee it up. Surprisingly, I crush it down the middle with a slight draw!

Man, I still love this game... How about you?

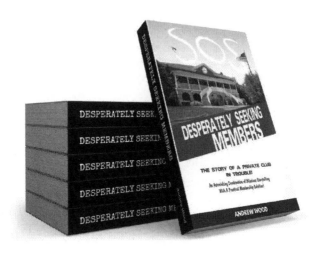

**Also by Andrew Wood, an excerpt from**

***Desperately Seeking Members.***

*The Story of a Private Club in Trouble!*

# Chapter 1

## What Do I Know About Membership Marketing?

## (Current Active Members: 252)

Hi, my name is Harvey McLintock, General Manager of Royal Oaks Country Club, located not far from your home, although you'd hardly notice for, other than the three-story waterfalls at both sides of the gates, the entrance is very discreet.

My folks named me after two characters in their favorite cowboy movies, neither of whom matched their surnames. Strange, I know, but better than being named after a couple of ghouls from a horror flick.

For twenty-two years I've worked in the private club business so I know a thing or two about how to get along with strange or difficult people. At work I put up the facade of a proper gentleman.

But the truth of the matter is I grew up around the docks in between caddie jobs and college, so I'm going to tell it just the way it really is at my club without any pretense.

If that's a little too up-front for some of you, I apologize, but I'm going to be brutally honest about my club because I know that it will help you at yours.

## What do I know about membership marketing?

To be honest, nothing!

I have never had to do any marketing, but as the club manager it's now become my job to help my new membership director reach her goals. That's easier said than done since she couldn't sell a dog a bone but, on the plus side, she does have the full support of the Board behind her, especially the president's and especially on Thursday night. You see "Poker Night" to Judge Henry Sutherland is pronounced "Poke Her" night and doesn't involve much card playing, if you get my drift...

She's been hired by the board to get membership back up to 400 where it needs to be so these rich old geezers don't have to chip in at the end of the year or, heaven forbid, let us increase the dues 5%.

Problem is, we only have 252 members and we're losing 'em faster than we can get 'em in. In fact, I forgot Al Bronson died yesterday so make that 251 members. At least this loss wasn't our fault; meaning we didn't piss him off so bad he quit!

The Board has formed a membership committee and they are "exploring the issue." I love that, don't you? We've lost 150 frigging members and the committee is still exploring the issue to see if we have a problem.

That, my friends, is where I take up my story...

**Active Members: 251**

**Join Harvey amid the chaos as he tries desperately, to turn the things around, in Desperately Seeking Members available on Amazon or desperatelyseekingmembers.com**

# ABOUT THE AUTHOR

## Andrew Wood Is the World's Leading Expert on Golf Marketing

With over 20 years' experience, working with over 3,000 clubs, in twenty different countries no single person in the golf industry has help more clubs or resorts increase their revenues. From small mom and pop operations to multi-million dollar resorts Andrew has developed winning strategies to increase play, outings, membership and room nights in North America, Europe, Africa, The Caribbean and Asia.

Born in Oxford, England and growing up in the Midlands near Shrewsbury, Andrew Wood immigrated to America in 1980 to peruse a career as a professional golfer. Unfortunately lack of talent held him back and he accidentally found himself running a small karate school in Southern California. After struggling to survive for 18 months as a small business owner he decided to focus all his attention on marketing. This focus soon paid off and he quickly increased his income to six figures while still in his twenties.

His initial interest in marketing turned into a passion and he quickly turned the single school into a national franchise of over 400 units. After selling out of the karate business in the late 90's he moved to Florida where he founded Legendary Marketing, a business designed to combine his passion for golf and travel with his marketing expertise. Legendary quickly built a name for itself in the golf industry with the early adoption of websites, social media and email marketing.

Author of over 40 sales, marketing and personal development books including; Legendary Advice, Making Your Business the One They Choose, **Cunningly Clever Marketing, Legendary Selling, Cunningly Clever Entrepreneur** and The Golf Marketing Bible, The Hotel & Resort Marketing Bible and **The Golf Sales Bible.**

He is considered the world's leading expert in golf, resort and real estate marketing and spoken to thousands of audiences worldwide on the topics from his books.

If you would like to increase your revenue contact him directly, he does still answer his own emails ☺

**Contact: Andrew Wood, Directly @**

Andrew@LegendaryMarketing.com

# OTHER BOOKS BY ANDREW WOOD

*Legendary Advice—101 Proven Strategies to Increase Your Income, Wealth & Lifestyle*

*Legendary Achievement—How to Maximize Your True Potential & Live the Life of Your Dreams*

*Cunningly Clever Marketing*

*Cunningly Clever Entrepreneur*

*Legendary Selling*

*Legendary Leadership*

*Making Your Business the One They Choose*

*The Traits of Champions* (with Brian Tracy)

*The Joy of Golf*

*The Golf Marketing Bible*

*The Golf Marketing Bible Vol. 2*

*The Hotel & Resort Marketing Bible*

*The Golf Sales Bible*

*How to Make $150,000 a Year Teaching Golf*

*Confessions of a Golf Pro*

*Desperately Seeking Members* (as Harvey S. McKlintock)

*Cowboy Leadership (With Pat Parelli)*

## Micro Books 30—Minutes to Legendary Leadership Series

*Legendary Vision*

*Legendary Passion*

*Legendary Confidence—How to Build It in Yourself and Others*

*Legendary Trust*

*Legendary Strategy*

*Legendary Action*

*Legendary Communication*

*Legendary Charisma—How to Get It!*

*Legendary Problem Solving & Creativity—How to Remove Any Obstacle*

*Legendary Motivation*

*Legendary Courage*

*Legendary Persistence*

## Legendary Entrepreneur Series

*Legendary Service—How to Give It!*

*Legendary Innovation—How to Unleash It!*

*Legendary Problem Solving—How to Remove Any Obstacle*

*Legendary Management—How to Deliver Fast Results!*

*Legendary Start-Ups—How to Start & Grow a New Business*

*Available at  www.AndrewWoodInc.com*

Andrew Wood

Made in the USA
Middletown, DE
04 August 2019